Love's Encore

by

Kathleen Ann Gallagher

Love's Encore

Cover Art by *Diana Carlile*

The Wild Rose Press, Inc.
PO Box 708
Adams Basin, NY 14410-0708
Visit us at www.thewildrosepress.com

Publishing History
First Edition, 2022
Trade Paperback ISBN 978-1-5092-4423-2
Digital ISBN 978-1-5092-4422-5

Previously Published by Beachwalk Press
Published in the United States of America

He gave her the cutest smile that made her shiver. It was as if she'd told him the secret to the universe. Vince put the menu on the bed. He reached for her, gently took hold of her shoulders, and pulled her close. This time, the kiss was hot and heavy. His fingers trailed along her back, and each stroke made her temperature rise. The sound of her heart beating pounded in her ears as she melted into his strong arms. Who needs food?

"I didn't bring you up here to seduce you," he said, his tone deep, yet low.

"I know, Vince. It's been a long time coming." Sadie sighed as she held his gaze. She wasn't going to miss out on the opportunity to be with Vince. Life was far too short. She had first-hand experience. She was one of the lucky ones. A few of the friends she'd made in the oncologist office weren't as fortunate. They'd lost their battle.

He rested his hand on her thigh. "Do you mean it? If you'd rather grab something in the food court, I'd go along with you."

"I'm fine. I've changed my mind about eating."

"It's funny, now that you mention it, so have I. All of the excitement from the show and then being with you. I'm one privileged man." He cradled her face in his hands and moved up close. His lips found hers and locked into an embrace. She uttered a soft moan.

Her decision to push fear aside, along with the gift of a full recovery, gave Sadie the green light to move forward. She smiled and raised her hand to Vince's chest and massaged it, going in circles.

Praise for Kathleen Ann Gallagher

"First, I would like to thank the author Kathleen Ann Gallagher for giving me this book for an honest review. I enjoyed reading this book. The story-line is good and the world building nicely done. The characters are well developed and written. I am looking forward to reading more from this author. "

~ Dalene rated it really liked it

Dedication

This book is dedicated to my children Dina, Anthony, and Jake. I am forever grateful for their love and support.

Chapter 1

When a steady round of indecipherable sounds blared across the speakers and the plane rocked from side to side, the hair on Sadie's arms stood up. Chattering broke out among the passengers. Was something wrong? Tension began in her jaw. With her eyes shut tight, she began the Hail Mary.

She forced a breath as soon as the cracking ceased. The pilot uttered a sincere sounding apology and announced he was preparing to land. The front of the plane tilted downward, and she gripped the armrest. She rested her head back. The tiny pillow molded to her neck. A rippling started in her stomach, and as she held her breath, the plane shook. A rocky descent wasn't about to change her mood. A few tears filled her eyes. After the year she'd endured, nothing was going to stop her. It had taken time to for her muster up the courage to move forward, however she'd embraced the things that mattered.

Sadie reached into her red patent leather bag, took out a tissue, and patted her cheeks. Raccoon eyes wouldn't match her pretty cobalt blue jacket. Recollections of when she was a teenager, sitting in the family room and watching the Oscars with her parents, flashed in her head. She'd finally made it to California. She had to admit the allure of her favorite celebrities as they strolled down the red carpet never got old. It was exhilarating to say the least. Her heart flip-flopped in anticipation of a week with two of the most caring people she'd ever met, her best friends. Their generous offer to take her on a much-needed girls vacation to celebrate the end of her chemotherapy had kept her from giving up during the difficult days.

The worst year of her life was finally over. With an open mind and a grateful heart, she anticipated each new opportunity. A second chance was a gift. This time around, she'd relish in what life had to offer. It was a blessing how well-being had replaced a relentless sense of doom. A celebratory trip with her best friends was merely the beginning of a bright new chapter. Cancer didn't win. Maybe she was a little too positive, if that was at all possible. *LA, here I come!*

"Are you okay?" Millie asked as she tapped Sadie lightly on her arm.

"I'm wonderful," she immediately responded. Nothing could come close to the feeling of relief when her doctor had announced she was cancer free. The dark cloud over her head had finally lifted. "These are happy tears." Sadie grabbed her friend's hand and gave a squeeze. Gratitude settled deep into her heart. "I'm so excited. My friends are the best." She held a thumb up and smiled.

Millie snuggled up close. "You deserve it."

Sadie chuckled to herself. Millie was the motherly type, and Sadie appreciated the way her friend always listened to her when she spoke, unlike Jill, who liked to be the center of attention. Nevertheless, she adored them both. Tall and slender with long auburn hair, Millie carried herself with the grace of a high fashion model, and her gentle and caring nature fit the role of pre-school teacher. Jill was all of five feet, but she knew how to take control of a room. Those big brown eyes, sleek black Sassoon haircut, and the comedic way she told a story gripped 'em every time. Sadie realized wholeheartedly that Jill's hilarious take on life at the strangest times had helped her cope after surgery. They were a unique threesome for sure. Although different, they complimented each other perfectly.

"You sure do, honey," Jill joined in. Her dangling silver earrings swayed as she gave a nod. "Land this baby and let the fun begin." She tugged on the strap on her seatbelt and it snapped tight. "You're a real doll, and we love you."

"I love you too. Both of you. We all deserve a vacation. We've been through so much together." Sadie settled low in her seat. She closed her eyes again and said a silent thank you.

When she opened them, the comfort of her gal pals arms laced through hers made her smile. Clarity came at a price, however difficult. Maybe she was being emotional, but her unexpected illness had allowed her to see things more clearly. The tiny space of the three-seat row was a safe cocoon, and as she observed the breathtaking scenery outside the window, she let out a peaceful sigh. Cottony white clouds moved aside, as if to allow her to see the cavernous space below.

She wasn't going to let an opportunity to explore new adventures pass her by. Things wouldn't have gone so smooth if she hadn't had Millie and Jill by her side. Close to her heart stood each milestone they'd shared. How else would they get through first loves, breakups, family crisis, and most importantly, summer breaks?

A diagnosis of breast cancer wasn't going to define

her. Instead, she rallied and took it on with a vengeance. Although her scars from a lumpectomy had healed well, her emotional state of mind had gone through a whirlwind of changes. Sadie gained comfort knowing how her mother had beat it. Her pride for the brave woman increased with each year, not only for the way she excelled in the hospital as an emergency room nurse, but instead of feeling sorry for herself during treatment, she had developed and nurtured an undeniable passion for photography.

Hopefully, she'd find the perfect piece to add to her mom's collection of sea shells on vacation. There was nothing like living at the beach. Even though travel gave her a lift, her little cottage nestled a few blocks from the beach was where she found solace. She'd never settle for life without the scent of the sea air, a group of friendly neighbors, the sand between her toes, and the ocean breeze.

A few more bumps made her stomach flip, but she endured.

Jill closed her eyes, and Millie bit the side of her mouth.

"We'll be fine." Sadie gave them each a pat on the leg.

She reached down into her purse to search for a mint, and lifted out a worn-out get well card from her students. A small token, signed by all of them, yet she'd appreciated it. What a thoughtful gesture. The other things she'd taken for granted, like ice cream, morning coffee, trips to the hair salon, and shopping on a Saturday afternoon, all seemed like a special treat now. With a busy life, the simple things had taken a back seat. Not anymore.

Sadie found a packet of mints, opened the top, and popped one in her mouth, then carefully slid the card into a large side pocket and zipped it up. She took out a pocket mirror, flipped it open, rearranged her long, swooping bangs, and fluffed up the rest of her trendy, short hair. The lighter shade of blonde her hairdresser had convinced her to try went well with her hazel eyes. Optimism surged through her body as if she'd won the lottery. No more fretting over things like whether she'd ever get a raise, or letting schedules get in the way of living in the moment. Sadie craned her neck to get a glimpse of the magnificent view of LA, and she chewed on her bottom lip. *We made it.*

The wheels of the plane hit the ground smoothly, and as she exhaled, Sadie put her hands together in prayer. What a relief to have made it safe and sound. She wasn't afraid to fly, but with all of the commotion, it was good to be on the ground. Six hours of sitting still wasn't in her skillset. Sadie knew it'd be a long day, due to the time difference, but she looked forward to every minute of this fabulous adventure. Juggling a small overnight bag, she stood, awaiting the line of passengers as they lined the aisle.

"Hurry, here's our chance." Jill tugged Sadie's sleeve.

They giggled as they shoved one another like happy kids at an amusement park. Sadie's heart skipped a beat. What a thrill to be headed to a great hotel where she could lounge at the pool, instead of lying around feeling like crap. A clean bill of health had to be taken seriously. Things had the potential of turning out so much worse.

"Tommy must miss me already. He's texting me a

step-by-step account of his day," Jill blabbed as she rolled her eyes and pushed a strand of hair behind her ears, her heels clicking on the ramp to the airport. "I'm so over his smothering and his immature attitude and need to control me. In reality, I'm in the driver's seat."

"Don't complain, Jill. You're lucky to be one step ahead of him at all times." Millie gave a confident nod as she ran her hand along the side of her perfectly pressed pants. "Mine is probably glad he's free for the week. This way he can veg out after work in his shorts and order take-out. I think he likes it better when I'm not around."

Sadie admired Jill's bubbly disposition and the way it was reflected in her style. A pair of dark blue designer jeans, a crisp white shirt, and shiny red shoes, along with a matching belt made her stand out in a crowd. Unlike herself, who usually preferred a more conservative approach to fashion, until most recently. In the past, it was important to her to always look professional. You never knew when you might be faced with a networking situation. Her transformation had begun with the trip. She was proud of the way she paired up a cute pair of tan capris with a taupe sleeveless shirt and a form-fitting sweater. Change was a good thing.

"We all agreed that this week is a girls' event. It's all about us. Remember?" Sadie kept her voice low, not wanting to sound bossy.

"You're right," Millie said.

Jill shook her head and gave a mischievous grin. "Hmm…"

"Promise you won't laugh when you see me in my new bikini." Sadie grinned.

Maybe if she had a guy of her own, she'd feel differently, but maybe not. There wasn't time for a serious relationship. The life of a drama teacher didn't end when the bell rang. With the spring production of *Pippin* being cast as soon as she got back, her focus was her work. It had been her whole world. For a second, she found herself back in line, waiting to read for Miss Nolan for the lead in the senior play. The role fit her like a glove. Sadie shook her head to free herself of the memories. What was the point in reliving the past? It wasn't meant to be. Back to reality.

"This is our chance to walk around with no makeup, relax on the beach, shop 'til we drop, if we feel like it, and eat dessert every night. Okay, we can shave our legs. But no worrying about your relationships. Those are the rules." Sadie stood in line to pick up her luggage. While she waited for her bags to arrive, she checked her messages.

"Finally. There's our stuff. Come on, you two."

She nearly collided with a person who had the same idea as she jolted to retrieve her belongings. "Excuse me." When she saw the irritated look on the woman's face Sadie decided to wait her turn, and she stepped aside. Time was too valuable to waste it arguing.

Once the girls grabbed their luggage, Jill flagged down an attendant, and he came over and piled the bags on a cart. Sadie picked up the pace as they headed out of the airport. Life had been on hold long enough. She'd placed her teaching career high on the priority list and let her own need sometimes take a back seat. It was all about balance. A half-year on the sofa in her fluffy slippers and soft pajamas had forced her to look deep inside.

A limo driver holding a sign with *Layne* in big, bold letters waited near the exit. "Here's our ride," Sadie eagerly announced.

"You go, girlfriend," Jill bolstered as she cracked her chewing gum.

Once they boarded the shiny, black car she'd previously arranged, Sadie peered out of the window, not wanting to miss a thing. It wouldn't be long before she dug her toes in the white sand at the beaches. She'd convinced her friends they should do their own thing instead of booking with a travel agent. They'd accumulated magazines and books on Los Angeles and the surrounding areas. It was better to be spontaneous and seize the moment.

She opened her top button and ran a hand across her neck, welcoming the warmth as the beams of bright sun hit the back seat through the open sunroof. After a brutal winter stuck indoors, she was eager to peel off her layers and expose a little skin. She couldn't wait to slip into her new, hot pink bathing suit. The few extra pounds she'd put on last fall came off during the long winter on chemo. She wasn't complaining, but now that she was able to exercise, the process of toning up had begun.

Her cheeks tingled from smiling so much, and her heart nearly leaped out of her chest.

"Okay, ladies. Here we are," the driver announced as he peeked in the rearview mirror.

The middle-aged man with olive colored skin and a friendly face, dressed in office casual attire, had made a good impression. His driving skills topped most of the cab drivers back home. He pulled over to the curb, hopped out, and opened the back door.

He pulled a business card out of his pocket and handed it to Sadie. "If you need a ride, I'd be glad to accommodate. It's not easy to find your way in the city."

"I'm not sure what we're doing. Thank you." Sadie hesitated, but she had to admit it was something to think about.

"I have discounted rates for a group," he happily added.

"That's great. Thank you." She slipped him a generous tip.

Sadie turned and stared up at the huge hotel. "This place is in a prime spot in the heart of LA. Did you see the theater we passed?" She held one arm out. "I've seen some of the award shows televised from in there." It was surreal to be in front of the place where academy award nominees had stopped for interviews before the show. She squinted and slipped on her sunglasses. The warm breeze lifted her bangs, and she quickly ran her fingers along them. "I can feel the difference in the air." She drew in a breath. Life couldn't get any better.

A young man wearing a white shirt with the hotel's name on his lapel pushed a large cart. He smiled as he piled on their luggage and led the way inside.

"I can't believe this place. Do you see the cars dropping people off? Big bucks. I feel like a celebrity." Jill stood tall and began a confident strut up to the entrance.

"You look like one too," Sadie remarked as she curled her lips up and mimicked a whistle.

Together, they entered a lobby grand enough to suit a queen. A huge, gold water fountain graced the main room. Modern chandeliers added an air of sophistication. Shiny, white floors made the entrance warm and inviting. They approached a rounded, granite front desk with a smiling staff dressed in tailored, navy blue jackets. The sweet scent of fresh flowers welcomed them.

"I can't wait to see our room." Millie's eyes were as wide as sand dollars.

"This place is too good to be true." Jill turned her head back and forth like a wind-up doll.

Sadie took charge at the desk. Someone needed to be in control. Even though she tried to appear calm and collected on the outside, her mind raced with a detailed list of all the places she wanted to visit. The little tourist book on LA her mother had given her sat on the coffee table, and it became her go-to whenever she needed a reminder of what was around the corner. She'd memorized it from cover to cover. Her blood shot through her veins, sending her nerve endings hopping.

A young man smiled as he assisted her with the check-in. "Enjoy your stay, Ms. Layne."

"Oh, I will. Thank you." Sadie strutted across the lobby with adrenaline surging through her body.

The buzzing of tourists making their way through the entryway made it seem like Christmas, and she never wanted this feeling to end.

"Let's stop for coffee." Sadie hadn't had her caffeine quota for the day. And besides, this trip was about spontaneity.

"Good idea. I sure could use a pick-me-up." Jill trotted ahead and led the way to the coffee shop in the middle of the atrium.

The wide open area lined with pretty greenery and

bright orange tables with padded matching chairs was crowded. People gathered around in small groups, some with their laptops. Many of them wore name tags with a romance writer's logo on them. A sign in front of a wide hallway announced a writer's conference. It didn't bother Sadie. It made the place more exciting. She scanned her surroundings as they ordered their favorite specialty drinks.

"I'm dying for a mocha latte with mounds of whipped cream on top. Give me sweets." Sadie's mouth watered as she shuffled her feet and wiggled her hips.

"You're craving sugar like you haven't had any in days." Jill always told it like it was.

"Sorry, I'm giddy over finally being here." Sadie's head spun as she raised her shoulders. She took a deep breath. The type of anxiety she was experiencing was the good kind, perfect for enhancing your senses.

"The time difference will do that to you, but it's worth it. We're going to have a blast." Jill picked up the tray and carried their coffees to a sitting area. "Let's check out the place from down here." She stopped to grab a couple of napkins from the counter. "We should have been born rich. I could get used to staying in places like this."

"You're a nut, but I love you," Sadie said as she followed her.

"Wait for me," Millie shouted. "I was drooling over the cupcake display," she confessed, licking her lips.

Jill's heel wobbled and she tripped as Millie rushed to meet up with them.

Sadie jumped in to break her fall. "Be careful." Jill's slip and fall reminded Sadie of a Miss America toppling over onstage in a pair of stilettos. "Are you okay?" She took hold of Jill's arm.

"I'm fine." Jill gave a sigh. "Maybe I should have worn my flats."

"Here, sit down." Sadie placed her bag down and pulled out a chair. She waited until her friend sat, and then she plopped in the seat beside her. Millie joined them.

"This place is prettier than I'd expected. It's larger too. I'm thrilled to be here with you both," Sadie said. "Now, this is what I call a scrumptious splurge," Sadie said, gingerly lifting the lid. A big dollop of luscious, white fluffy whipped cream, laced with a touch of cinnamon, made her mouth water. Heavenly. "I've missed you so," she proclaimed as she put her fingertips together and kissed them. "Perfection!"

Nothing had tasted good while she was on chemo, and she hadn't been able to tolerate anything cold or enjoy a cup of coffee. She sipped her latte, as happy as a hippie in the wild; her spirit was free.

"We made it." Sadie raised her coffee cup.

"Friends forever," Jill toasted. She took a gulp of her drink, crinkled up her nose, and rubbed her stomach. Her complexion faded from peachy to pale. "I can't believe I'm getting cramps."

"What a bummer. I'm so tired I could drop," Millie added as she let out a yawn. "Go figure. Do you think a strong cup of coffee would help? I guess it's all the hype of traveling. Hopefully, I'll be as good as new after a shower." She straightened her shoulders and gave a tiny grin.

"No time for whining. This is our vacation. I urged you two to try to get a full night's sleep before we got on the plane. Come on, let's go up to our room, and I'll tuck you both in for a nap." It may have sounded like a joke, but she wanted her friends to make a speedy recovery. There wasn't a minute to waste. Sadie stood, gathered the empty cups, and tossed them in a nearby trash receptacle.

On the way upstairs, she stopped at the desk and asked for the bellhop to bring up their luggage. She pushed her bag up on her shoulder and walked with her friends to the elevator. Plush gray and burgundy carpet led the way to a hallway with lovely gold sconces that added to the ambience. An alluring floral scent surrounded the area. Oversized, undressed windows at the end of the hall allowed a glimpse of the glorious city.

When they arrived at their room, the bellhop was waiting for them. "Great, our luggage got here before we did." Sadie opened her change purse and took out a few dollars. She handed it to the young man.

"Thank you. Do you need anything else?"

"I think we're good for now."

He nodded then made his way down the hall and slipped around the corner.

"What a little hot tamale," Jill said as she stood behind the girls.

Sadie turned and gave her a light pinch on the arm.

"Ouch," Jill chirped.

"Be good." Sadie slipped the card in the slot on the door.

Once they were inside, her friends scurried in opposite directions.

Sadie's jaw dropped as she stared out of the wall of windows. "Would you look out here?"

She went over to the window in a trance-like state, her body as light as a ballerina's. A magnificent backdrop of the city of Los Angeles was right outside for their enjoyment. The Hollywood sign sat on the hills, and it was an enthralling focal point with the glistening sun offering a stream of light into their room. A clear, bright blue sky allowed an unobstructed view.

"I get the side of the bed closest to the window." She put in her bid and moved over to the entertainment center and turned on the radio. She turned to find Millie's suitcase sitting in the corner, and Jill was slouched in an arm chair with her feet on top of an ottoman.

Invigorated and ready to get the trip started, Sadie rolled up her sleeves and hurried to get organized. She hummed along with *It's My Life* by Bon Jovi playing on the radio as she reached deep into the side pocket of her suitcase.

"I have the task of unpacking down to a science, since the last time we went on a trip, when I spent more time ironing than sight-seeing." Fortunately, the closet was huge and stocked with plenty of hangers. Once she'd finished and slid her luggage in a corner hideaway, she was ready to explore the hotel.

Jill had already curled up in the chair under a chenille throw, and Millie was tucked in bed, the covers up to her neck, with her eyes half-closed.

"You've got to be kidding. Right?"

The dark circles under Millie's eyes popped out from under her foundation, and it looked like she'd been up for days. Jill moaned as she held a pillow against her belly.

"It looks like I'm going out by myself." Sadie

stared down at them with her shoulders slumped. She sighed and shook her head, disappointed but determined. "All right. Feel better." She opened the door and turned around to face them. "Do you want me to bring you back anything?"

A couple of headshakes were all the pooped-out pair could muster.

"I'll be downstairs checking it out if you need me." She was off. By the size of the place, she was bound to find something of interest to keep her busy while her friends rested. Although, she wouldn't venture too far off path without them.

The elevator made the journey down as quickly as a roller coaster. When she stepped out, a beautiful upscale restaurant caught her eye. A crystal clear glass entryway led the way to a grand room with high back leather booths, lovely vintage pottery filled with fresh flowers, and intimate, tastefully adorned tables. Sadie wandered over to take a look at the menu posted on the outside and she made a mental note to make a reservation. She'd budgeted for this celebration, and no-frills dining was definitely not the way to go. Millie and Jill's generosity in insisting on a gift of the plane fare was more than she'd dreamed of.

An extra wide hallway in the far right corner of the lobby housed an aisle with all types of items scattered on them. She'd noticed it when they'd first arrived. Now was the ideal time to sneak a close peek. Posters of book covers sat on easels and tables with magnets, calendars, pens, candy, and bookmarks that enticed her. She stopped alongside a display with candies wrapped in clear paper and tied with a red bow, and picked up a booklet with an eye-catching, bright blue cover.

As she flicked through it a couple of women with lanyards around their necks stood beside her, smiled, and loaded up their bags. The space suddenly got crowded, and she edged her way to the end of the display table. She scanned a shiny postcard of a bare-chested man with thick, black hair. He held a woman around the waist as they stood side by side. Heat formed on her cheeks. The cover model looked familiar.

After focusing, she raised her hand to her face, her mouth dropping open. She had no idea Vince from her theater workshop was a model, and she couldn't take her eyes off his chest. He was good looking, but his body had changed. He'd added a six-pack since she'd last seen him without a shirt, when they used to hang out down by the water back home in Point Pleasant Beach.

Sadie picked up the promo card with Vince's photo on front, turned it over, and read the book blurb. It sounded intriguing, and she actually considered reading a romance by the pool. A sign on a stand at the beginning of the aisle listed the times for a book fair open to the public. If she had time, she'd stop by. Falling in love wasn't something she'd thought about lately, but after she read the teaser, she had second thoughts. It had been a long time since she'd felt a pair of strong arms around her.

Her ex-boyfriend, Aiden, didn't really count. She was glad the fellow teacher had finally gotten the hint and moved on. She'd resigned to the fact that they were only two people who had kept each other company while they waited for the right person to come along. Lately, she'd rather throw on a pair of fuzzy slippers and a cozy robe and watch television with a bowl of popcorn on a Saturday evening.

She inconspicuously slipped a few of the freebie items into her bag and snuck a peek over her shoulder. You never knew when a bag clip or jar opener would come in handy. Friendly glances and cordial hellos from the people in the downstairs area of the hotel helped her let go of the awkwardness that took hold of her emotions. By the looks of the others without badges loading up on the goodies, she realized the promotion hallway was open to the public.

Out of the corner of her eye, she spotted a small crowd gathered around someone standing next to one of the ballroom entrances. Sadie wandered over to get a glimpse. When the group cleared, she moved closer and found her old theater classmate standing in front of an oversized easel. It housed an advertisement for what looked like a television show. He was here in person. Vince De Carlo had been working out. He'd transformed into a different person since they'd performed together at the neighborhood theater. She'd felt the same old twinge in her gut when they ran into one another at the reunion, but who knew that under his clothes he had such an amazing body? He'd never mentioned a thing about posing for a romance cover. Anyway, it was his business.

She steadied herself and tried to focus. Tremors began in her hands, and she started a round of abdominal breaths before she got closer. Why was she so nervous? She'd given up on him years ago. If he'd wanted to ask her out, he would have.

Inching her way closer to the hunky, dark-haired man, she moistened her lips. She practically drooled once she got close enough to get a glimpse of his dazzling blue eyes. Her gaze dropped to his muscular thighs, admiring the way the tight pair of designer jeans hugged them just right. His crisp, white shirt was opened enough to let her sneak a peek at his chest, and her knees nearly buckled.

What the heck was happening? Was she getting a flu or were her desires resurfacing? She never expected to be overcome with hidden emotions. This was supposed to be a girls' getaway, yet she was still young, and after all, it was the season for romance. Maybe all of the smoldering images scattered around the lobby stirred something inside of her.

Sadie shook off the nerves, straightened her posture, and sucked her stomach in. Her new motto was taking chances and living life to the fullest. *Here goes.* She slowly approached her old theater partner. Hopefully he'd be happy to see her, and she wouldn't make a fool out of herself in the middle of an upscale hotel. Her heart picked up speed and a hot flash hit her hard.

"Hi, Vince. I'm surprised to run into you here." She offered a big smile. Relief washed over her when his expression brightened. Hopefully he didn't notice her schoolgirl jitters.

"Sadie Layne. I can't believe it." He smiled back at her and held his hands out. "I haven't seen you since the reunion last year."

"I know. It was great to get together with the old gang. I can't believe we graduated over ten years ago."

Small talk was a good start for now. Vince leaned in and gave her a friendly embrace. She hadn't expected that. He held onto her shoulders as he pulled back and stared intently. Goosebumps formed on her arms. She tried to hold it together and appear calm, but her insides jumped around like popcorn in a microwave.

"What brings you to LA?" Vince asked.

"I'm here on vacation with my friends." Her stare locked onto his heart-shaped lips and she shivered.

His huge smile and the admiring way his sexy blue eyes took on a gleam gave her an inkling that he was pleased to see her too. Who knew? He'd never expressed an interest other than a friendship. They did enjoy each other's company and they had a lot in common, but she had her doubts about being involved with a fellow actor, even though she'd had her longings. She'd heard horror stories about relationships in the business. Her work had been more important than a love affair.

Although, she did recall the passionate punch in his kiss. At the time, she thought it was his great acting skills. Could it have been real? She'd never forgotten when another classmate, Monica Sears, had cornered her and drilled her about the details of the love scene in the show. She'd always known why. Vince was one sexy dude.

"It's awesome to see you, Sadie. You look beautiful." He gave her a long, hard stare and flashed his pearly white smile. A dimple appeared on his cheek, and it took her over the edge.

The same adorable grin. Her head spun, and she took a few deep breaths. "You too." She reached into her bag and took out the cover flap with his picture on it. "When did you start modeling?"

He crossed his arms and chuckled. "Oh, you found out my dirty little secret?" His cheeks took on a reddish glow. "I got involved with the industry a couple of years ago. It got me through in between gigs," he admitted as he shrugged.

"I think you're a natural. Your pose made me want to read the story." His shirtless chest had a lot to do with her interest, but she'd keep it to herself. "What is this you have here?" Sadie pointed at the poster, trying to steady her trembling fingers. She'd like to believe her excitability was due to the anticipation of the trip, along with the long flight. But she knew that wasn't what had caused it.

The earthy scent of his cologne floated her way, and she'd had enough of this distraction, but she'd be polite. She was in LA to celebrate, not fool around.

"It's a pilot show we're pitching, and I scored the male lead." He curled up his fist and pumped it. "Yes! Can you believe it? We're filming the pilot episode tonight, and we're looking for audience members to fill the theater," he said, his expression beaming with pride. He took on a stance of confidence with his feet planted firmly on the floor, legs slightly spread, shoulders back, and his head high. You'd think he was a serviceman about to salute an officer.

"That's fabulous. It looks like you're finally on your way," she cheered, and offered him a congratulatory hug. He held onto her for a few minutes, and she didn't expect to enjoy it so much. Was her teenage crush turning into something much more?

"Why don't you try to come to the show tonight? I know it's short notice and you probably have plans, but if you can make it, it'd be great." He tilted his head, and she couldn't resist those alluring gray-blue eyes. "Sorry, I don't even know who you're here with. When did you get in?" Vince took a step back.

Out of the blue, this handsome, muscular, and confident looking man had caught her off guard and filled her head with naughty visions. Sadie held back a grin. She'd kept her cravings hidden when they'd hung out. Besides, it probably would have destroyed their friendship and ability to work together. But Sadie had to admit she loved his pouty lips. Everything about Vince oozed sex appeal.

"I'm here with my friends, Jill and Millie, on vacation," she said.

"Well, think about coming tonight. I'd appreciate your critique." He handed her the show's info packet. "That is if you don't try to change the script. You used to improvise. I remember the time Miss Nolan stormed out of the room when you changed your lines." With a gleam in his eye, he laughed.

She was surprised that he remembered the details. It was nice to know he'd paid attention. What he didn't know was that the strict teacher was the reason she left the theater. Her mean-spirited words had cut like a knife. *You might want to consider another field.*

"Is Dina here with you?" she asked. "You seemed pretty serious when I saw you together on the dance floor at the reunion." Sadie wasn't holding back any punches. If he was seeing someone, she'd force all thoughts of romance out of her head.

Vince frowned and shook his head. "Nope. It didn't work out. It's all good. It was mutual," he admitted.

"I'll see if my friends want to tag along tonight. From the sound of this teaser, it looks interesting and funny. Is there room for three of us?" Sadie's mind raced with ways to convince them. She'd find a way to get them to agree to the viewing. It might not be a night out on the town, but after a long day, an upbeat show with a handsome lead was a better plan.

Butterflies filled her stomach and she steadied herself, trying to get a grip on her emotions. Anticipation of something more than friendship with Vince hit her hard. Tucked away in the corner of her heart was a place for Vince. It was now or never.

Vince smiled and nodded. "Of course. I'll be sure to have seats up front waiting for you and your friends."

"How nice of you." Sadie's heart skipped a beat. If Vince got any closer, she'd be in his arms. *Steady, girl.* She took a deep breath.

A couple of women stopped by and hovered around him like a bunch of groupies, screeching. While he handed out flyers, he flashed his wide smile. He worked the crowd like a pro.

Sadie moved aside and observed him, in awe at how drastically he'd changed since they had acted together. He obviously worked out hard to transform his once thin built. She recalled how, after rehearsals, he'd take off before the rest of the class most of the time, but in the summer he did tag along to the group's favorite hangout on Ocean Avenue. They'd all share a few beers and comment about one another's performance. Honest, yet at times brutal. It was all meant to help one another. She'd never forgotten how much he loved Al Pacino. He'd imitated his idol in a few of his memorable roles when they'd hung out, and he was pretty good at impersonations.

Once the ladies had moved on, Vince waved Sadie over.

She moseyed back to his side. "I didn't want to interrupt you and your fans." Sadie picked up a pamphlet from the table.

"I wish they were fans." He gave a hearty laugh. "So, tell me what you're doing now," he intently inquired.

"I'm still teaching drama at the high school in Point Pleasant. I've been there for eight years." She opened her purse and dropped the information inside.

"Hmm." Vince placed his hand on his chin. "I recall you mentioned it at the reunion, but I thought you were subbing. Do you have time to go on auditions? I know how much you loved the theater." He gave a sideways look and crossed his arms. "We didn't have much time to catch up with the whole gang together."

"No, I've given up that life. I'm in the real world now, full time." She sighed.

A knot formed in the pit of her stomach. The very mention of what she'd given up made her shudder. It still hurt, and Sadie wasn't going to offer any further explanations. She had decided it was time to grow up, face responsibilities, and give up pipe dreams. Not everyone was born to be a star. It was all right for some people, but not for her. She had a right to change her mind. Didn't she? She'd heard the same surprised tone in her mother's voice when she told her she was leaving the theater. Eventually she accepted it. Hopefully, she'd made her mom proud.

"I'm sorry. I mean… Oh, I'm an idiot for being rude." His face turned a light shade of red. "It's great that you're a teacher. I bet your students adore you."

"I know what you mean. Don't let it bother you." She brushed a strand of hair out of her eyes, finding his nervousness appealing. He was upset that he'd insulted her. Vince was still thoughtful and sweet.

"You were great as Sandy in Grease," he insisted.

His sweet comments only added to his appeal. "Aww. Thank you. You were wonderful as Danny. Perfectly cast."

"Oh, so you think I'm cool and charming?" Vince moved a little closer, his tone teasing. He turned to pick up a piece of paper from the floor.

Sadie's gaze zeroed in on his butt in his snug jeans. She didn't want to be rude, but she couldn't help but gawk. Her heart did a couple of flips. A warm flash of heat started at the top of her head and trickled down her body. She was grateful he didn't have mind-reading abilities. All of a sudden she was at a loss for words, so she cleared her throat. It took a few deep breaths to gain composure.

"How about it? Are you free tonight?"

"I'm...umm..." she stammered. "I have to see what my friends want to do. They did take me on this trip. I had a rough year, but I'm back and I'm healthy." Sadie clung to the strap of her purse.

"I'm glad you're okay. If you don't mind me asking, what happened?" He spoke in a softer tone as he stared intently into her eyes.

Coming face to face with Vince so unexpectedly and the rush of resurfaced emotions threw Sadie off-balance. She had wanted to put her illness behind her and enjoy the trip. Now, she was feeling uncertain about even bringing it up. After a long pause, she inhaled and opened up. She didn't have anything to hide. In fact, she was proud of her strength and endurance. "I had breast cancer." Sadie lifted her chin with pride. "Luckily, it hadn't spread. After a lumpectomy and chemotherapy, I'm stronger than ever." With a clenched fist, she cheered her victory. "My girlfriends and I are here to celebrate my good fortune and the end of my treatment."

"I'm so sorry." His eyes saddened as he reached for her hand and got close enough to offer another hug.

Pity was the last thing she wanted from Vince, but she enjoyed the way it felt to be close enough to feel his warm breath on her neck. The scent of leather and musk tantalized her senses. The quick brush of his hand across her back sent a jolt down her spine. There was no denying she was still unbelievably attracted to Vince, and this time she wasn't ignoring it. She'd never expected to run into her old theater buddy as she was about to embark on the next chapter of her life.

"The whole experience gave me a fresh perspective on things. I've learned to live life differently. To enjoy the time I have instead of waiting for something to make me happy. I'm living in the moment." She couldn't help but smile. It wasn't hard to be happy.

She did worry about the way her whole body tingled when Vince looked into her eyes. She traced the outline of his chiseled features with her eyes, down his lips, and then to his strong chin. His dazzling smile left her body limp. She felt the pull of her heart, causing her whole system to lose control. There was no way of stopping her desires. She told herself to let go and enjoy it.

"I like your philosophy. I agree completely." He shifted his weight and gave an affirming nod. "I had a buddy who was stricken ill and he lost everything in the process. He's fine now, but making different choices.

You know, going for what he wants, not letting life pass him by."

"I'm sorry to hear about your friend, but I'm glad he has another chance." She smiled. He'd reduced her to mush and she loved it. "I better get back upstairs. It may take some convincing to get Millie and Jill to get ready." She tilted her head and pouted her lips. Sadie tried not to flirt, but she couldn't help it.

"Does that mean you're coming tonight?" His enthusiasm was contagious. He sounded as if he'd gotten a nomination for an Emmy. A wide smile appeared on his face and his eyes held a sparkle.

Sadie couldn't contain her emotions. Her knees shook and her gut did flip-flops. She was excited for him, and she really wanted to go. "I can't promise, but I will do my best to make it. I'd love to see your show."

She turned to go upstairs. If she looked back, she knew she'd find him watching her. She was back in the game. She picked up a quick stride. Not that she'd ever really had any action, but she was up for being a little naughty. After seeing Vince's scorching hot body, her mind wandered to scenarios that shocked even her. She chuckled under her breath.

It was refreshing to see Vince still working in the business and how he never gave up his dreams. She knew how many struggling actors gave up, including herself. Not that she didn't enjoy teaching. But there was always a little voice in the back of her mind reminding her about the life she could have had if she'd only had what it took.

****

Sadie found her friends up and already in their bathing suits. "You two sure made a quick recovery."

Happy to have company, she tossed her purse on the bed and plopped down. With her feet up, she grabbed a soft throw pillow and propped it behind her head.

"What are you smirking about?" Jill crinkled her forehead as she moved closer and sat. "Okay, spill it."

"What? Can't a girl be happy?"

Her friend knew her all too well, but Sadie would rather wait to tell them the whole story. She was the one who insisted this was a girls' trip. No boyfriends allowed or frets over relationships. There was plenty of time for that back home. Tonight wasn't an actual date, but by the way the chemistry felt between them, her instincts told her something was cooking...and she couldn't wait.

"I caught the tail end. Did something happen when you went out?" Millie pulled out the desk chair and sat, offering a suspicious glare.

"Okay, here it is. I ran into an old friend downstairs in the lobby. He's filming the pilot for a television show tonight, and he invited all of us to attend."

"Who is it? Is he famous?" Millie asked, her eyes widened.

"Is that why you're glowing all of a sudden?" Jill stood and went over to pick up her bottled water from the end table. She opened it and took a sip. "We're waiting." She rested a hand on her hip.

"It's the guy I used to tell you about from my theater group. Back then you two were too busy to come to a performance. Remember?" She spoke so fast that hyperventilation seemed imminent.

"Sorry, we had every intention of making a show. Isn't that right, Millie?"

"Umm...Yes, of course," Millie stuttered.

"I recall you sort of liked him," Jill mused.

"Vince is still as good looking as ever." Sadie rubbed her hand to rid herself of the pins and needles. *It might be a good idea to slow down. Vince really knocked me for a loop.*

"And?" Jill moved closer, put her hands on her knees, and bent down to look directly at her. "Go on."

She held one hand up, palm out. Tension arose in her upper back. "All right, I've always had a thing for Vince, and I'm dying to go tonight." There, she said it. "Are you two busy bodies happy?"

She lowered her head, her muscles still tight. Her heart settled in her chest with the admittance of the truth. Sadie couldn't help but smile. She'd stuffed all thoughts of Vince away since they hadn't spent much time together at the class reunion. Was she expecting too much after so many years? They weren't kids sharing their dreams of making it big on the stage anymore.

"So, how about it?" Sadie asked.

"It sounds like a lot of fun. I can't wait to see the mystery man who added a pretty blush to your cheeks. I'm in," Jill chirped. "I guess you changed your mind about the no-relationship clause on our trip." She placed her hand on the side of her mouth and gave a little cackle. "I'm all for it."

"Boy, so am I. You don't run into a sexy guy every day." Millie's bold comment was out of character, but Sadie welcomed it.

"Let's go down by the pool and soak up some sun. We can grab something to eat while we get some color." Sadie couldn't wait to see Vince perform again. She shed her jacket, rushed to the dresser, pulled out her two-piece, and jolted into the bathroom to change. "Be out in a minute."

"We have to look our best to flirt with Vinnie Poo," Jill teased.

Chapter 2

Vince was motivated and optimistic as he stood outside the theater next to the poster of *The Mall People*. With his energy level high and his heart open to his old infatuation, it was easy to anticipate unlimited possibilities. The show had a unique concept, and it centered on the crazy antics of a group of people bonded together by their jobs at a local mall. The writers outdid themselves.

He was one lucky guy. A new show and another chance with the woman he'd never forgotten made his heart thump like a warrior's drum. He never imagined he'd run into Sadie Layne on his trip to LA. She'd stepped out of his dreams. Now that he'd seen her, he couldn't stop thinking about her. Not that she hadn't popped into his mind now and then. Back home, in the seashore town of Point Pleasant, New Jersey, whenever he'd ride past the playhouse where they'd shared the infamous kiss, his pulse still raced. The glorious moment was embedded in his memory. She was beautiful, talented, supportive, and everything he'd ever wanted in a woman. He'd appreciated her efforts to come early for rehearsal and read lines with him.

Vince had regrets over not making a serious attempt to take her out when he'd had the chance. At the time, he didn't have the confidence or much experience with the opposite sex. Sure, he dated, but never a girl like Sadie. She was out of his league.

Why had he listened to his friend Matt? He'd advised Vince to steer clear of Sadie, telling him that if he ever tried, she'd laugh in his face. Matt still lived in town, and he was on wife number two. Yeah, right…he knew.

The flow of people who stopped by to ask about the show was steady. Once the crowd thinned, an elderly couple approached, holding hands.

"How are you?" Vince offered them a welcoming smile, all the time thinking it must be nice to spend a lifetime with someone you love.

"Are you a movie star?" The white-haired woman stood beside Vince, clutching a purse that overpowered her tiny frame.

"No, but I am an actor. I'd like to invite you both to be members of the audience for a show I'm in."

"We'd love to attend, young man. You're very handsome. If you're in it, it will be a hit." She reached into her bag, took out a card, winked, and handed it to him. Vince offered another smile and gave her a leaflet.

"See you tonight." The woman blew him a kiss.

He chuckled as he scanned her card. *Mamie's Psychic Readings*. Unlikely, nevertheless, her kind words were appreciated.

The stars seemed to be lining up for him. Vince had learned a thing or two since he hung around with Sadie. The sweet tone of her voice and the way she offered him a demure grin as she'd checked him out made his insides rattle. There was no denying an electrifying attraction between them, and he wasn't letting her go this time.

Positive vibes kept him sharp and on his toes. The

long awaited uphill climb had begun. It was about time. The pilot fell into his lap, and then, a hot and desirable woman stepped out of his past. Life was finally going his way. Vince's energy level held steady as he handed out the rest of the brochures.

In between potential viewers, he took a break and downed a bottled water and a protein bar. Nutrition and hydration were important to maintain a healthy weight. His head buzzed as he sampled the sweet scent of Sadie's perfume she'd left behind on his shirt. He ran his hand across his abdomen. Hours of sweating and pumping iron at the gym had paid off. When he'd performed with Sadie in their last show together, he was all of one hundred and fifty pounds. A scrawny physique added to his insecurities back in the day. He'd worked hard to build muscle mass.

Vince was appreciative for the opportunity to star in *The Mall People*, but he wasn't going to get his hopes up too high. The show wasn't a shoo-in, and many of his comrades in the business had multiple pilots that had tanked. But deep in his gut he had a feeling this show was different. The producer was a true professional and totally invested in the project.

As Vince glanced over the colorful advertisement, he recognized the future held boundless promise. The countdown to a better life included Sadie, and now he had to show her how bad he'd always wanted her. She was the missing piece to the puzzle.

He took a deep breath and let it out slowly, his mind at ease. Nights spent eating peanut butter and jelly on stale English muffins were nearly coming to an end. It was a good thing he'd decided to hold onto a weekend position at Marseille's Restaurant on the beach. Between the modeling jobs and the tips at the waterfront restaurant, he'd been able to keep a roof over his head. Every little bit had helped to pay the rent on his run-down studio at the beach. Thank goodness a few network commercials had come along, and he always jumped at the opportunity. All thanks to his cigarette-smoking, joke-cracking, yet persistent agent, Joey G. He wouldn't have scored the role as Mickey, a rookie cop, in *The Mall People* without his unwavering agent.

A couple of stragglers passed by and Vince handed out the last of the invites. An overwhelming sense of appreciation found a place in his heart. A trial run of the pilot episode, scored by the public, was a step in the right direction. He crossed his arms and snuck a peek at his watch. It was time to pack up, grab something to eat, and prepare for the show. Vince slowly rolled up the poster and folded the easel.

His mind wandered to the soft feel of Sadie's skin when his lips had brushed her cheek, and his heart thumped in his chest with the very thought of her. The way she swayed her hips when she walked sent his blood soaring through his veins. Sadie carried herself like a woman who knew what she wanted, and it was an appealing quality. Her confidence and upbeat attitude, especially after all she'd been through, was tantalizing. It made him want her even more. His gut told him there was something unsettling in her life, besides her recent illness. Whatever it was, it was her business. One day she'd let him inside her heart and trust him enough to share her deepest fears.

Vince took a moment to go over the opening scene of the show in his head. In between the punch lines, he imagined Sadie's beautiful smile. It was hard to shift to work mode. He hadn't felt like this in a long time. He'd better pull himself together to perform this evening's show. Developing his craft had been first and foremost over the last few years.

His body felt wired and tingly when Sadie got close to him. Whatever the spell she cast over him, he was struck hard. He would score a date with Sadie while they were both in town for sure. Meeting across the map wasn't a coincidence. It was fate. He felt it in his bones.

He lifted the easel, tucked the poster under his arm, and took off toward the elevators.

The fire in his spirit had kept him on the right course up until now. He'd learned how to plan and put his best foot forward. In the back of his mind sat the image of him as a scared, young boy. He'd been through hell. One eviction notice after the next disrupted any sense of normalcy in the De Carlo household. Anger still boiled in his gut for the way his father had always lied about paying the bills on time and had drank away the rent money. But it only made him push harder. Nothing was going to hold him back. He was hungry for a better life, and Sadie was going to be part of it. Sure, she had an established career, a house, and all that came along in the real world of a successful thirty-year-old. His time would come. It just took a little longer. A twinge in his gut about how Sadie's life was at a different stage than his interrupted his upbeat state of mind, but he quickly dismissed it.

Vince held his head up and his shoulders back as he trotted through the lobby and up to his room. He'd touch base with the cast before show time. First things first. It was time to focus on his performance tonight.

This was his big chance, and he wasn't going to screw it up.

He made it upstairs, balancing the display in an attempt to avoid injuring anyone who got too close. Once inside, he stuck the easel in the corner and placed the artwork on the table, then left to go get some food. He'd found an organic shop one floor up when he scouted around earlier in the day.

The chicken salad with romaine lettuce looked good. His mouth watered from the aroma of the fresh grilled chicken and herbs. Vince placed his order.

The server wore a bright yellow apron with eye-catching white daisies around the borders. "Aren't you the guy who played in the beer commercial?"

"You recognized me without the cowboy hat," he teased, grinning at her.

"I sure do. I love that ad. I'll put in some extra chicken," she whispered.

The woman left to prepare his order, and Vince caught her as she peeked over her shoulder. Being recognized in public never got old.

His stomach growled as he waited, and he checked his messages. A string of good luck texts from his buddies at the gym and one from his mom made him smile. Stifled by the shock of seeing Sadie, he'd made the mistake of forgetting to exchange numbers with her.

While he waited for this order, he pondered his conversation with her and hoped she could convince her friends to come to the show. Everything had changed. His chance of winning Sadie's heart wasn't lost after all. It would be great to spend time alone with her afterward, but he didn't want to interrupt her plans with her friends. After all, it was a trip to celebrate. He'd find a way.

When the young woman returned with his order and handed it to him, her hands trembled. "Would you mind if I asked for your autograph?" she stammered.

He was touched by her request. "I wouldn't mind at all." He reached for the post-it pad she held. "What's your name?"

"Angel." She let out a squeal and jumped up and down. "Thank you so much."

"It's my pleasure. Here's some information about being an audience member for a television pilot we're filming." He gave her a handout with the info. "I hope you can make it. It's being filmed right here in the hotel. Our set is set up in a theater upstairs."

"I'll be there." She waved, wearing a bright grin.

Vince returned to his room. He grabbed a sparkling water from the tiny refrigerator and sat at the table by the windows. He opened the bottle and took a sip. As he began to eat, he stared out at the glorious hills and down at the highway. LA was a grand town, full of opportunity. It'd be a dream come true to have his footprints on the Hollywood Walk of Fame one day.

Somehow, after his meeting with Sadie, he wanted it even more. He was determined before, but today wasn't just an ordinary day. It carried so much more. Long gone were the days in his tiny bedroom in his mother's rented house and the way he'd stared at the posters of his idols on the wall. One day it would be his poster encouraging a young dreamer. It brought him joy to make people smile and entertain them, washing away their pain or sorrow. He drew in a deep breath. One day he'd help his mother get the life she deserved. Sadie never held it against him back in the day when the kids teased him about his father's drinking. He'd never forgotten how kind and accepting she was.

His cellphone vibrated in his pocket, and he reached for it. His manager's number flashed on the screen. "Hey, what's up?"

"I'm checking in on you. How's it going? Are you ready for tonight?" Joey asked.

"I'm more than ready, I'm going to knock it out of the park." Vince stood and moved over to the windows.

"Now that's what I needed to hear. I'm finishing up some paperwork, but I'll be there at ringside."

"Great! I'll catch up with you later, and thanks for everything."

Joey gave a harsh cough. "This warm weather is getting to me." He laughed. "I'm here for you, kid."

Vince sat back down and finished eating. If he didn't hurry, he'd be late. He peeled off his clothes and jumped into the shower. The warm water trickled down his head and onto his back, and it invigorated him. As his muscles relaxed, his mind wandered to Sadie and he had to turn the nozzle toward cold to combat his erotic thoughts. *Boy, this woman drives me out of my mind.* If she showed up tonight, it would be one hell of a treat all the way around.

He grabbed the terrycloth robe from the hook on the door, slipped it on, and went out to get his phone. He wanted to check on his co-star, Meg Talbot. She was as excited as him to be part of the team, and she'd already had a run in a hit show. With her along for the ride, the show had a better chance of making the cut.

****

Sadie had a bounce in her step as she led the way to an area where shiny white lounge chairs were lined

37

up next to a sparkling pool. Palm trees, tropical plants, and sections with yellow and white striped umbrellas gave it an upscale flare. She lifted her oversized sunglasses and couldn't believe what a gorgeous shade of blue the sky was. The scent of suntan oil came at her from all angles.

"I could get used to this." She held her face up to the sun. The warm rays brushed her skin, and she savored the burst of heat.

She inhaled the fresh air from the rooftop. With a panoramic view of LA, the pool area was the finest place in the hotel. Sadie had counted down the days on her calendar, with the trip being her light at the end of the tunnel.

After she dropped a beach bag on a nearby chaise, she slipped off her new beige fishnet cover-up. It was the moment she'd waited for. The big reveal. "How do you like it?" She held one hand on her hip.

A round of applause from her friends made her blush. "You look beautiful. The suit was made for you," Jill said.

"Thank you. Let's get wet, then bask in the sun all afternoon." Luckily, she'd remembered to bring sunblock. Her pretty turquoise dress wouldn't work to her advantage tonight if she looked like a lobster.

"I'm with you." Jill placed her tote on a side table, flipped her hair, paraded over to the pool stairs, and sat with her feet in the water. She glanced up at the tan, muscular lifeguard, and smiled.

Sadie joined her and spoke close to her ear. "What are you doing?" Jill was looking for trouble. She had a great guy back home, but Sadie knew how her friend liked to indulge in an occasional harmless flirtation.

"You know I love you and Tommy." She sighed. The last thing she wanted was to hurt her friend's feelings.

"Don't worry, I'll be good." Jill partially covered her mouth and whispered, "My man is never around. His job is his whole world."

"He's trying to build a future for the both of you, sweetie. I wish I had someone so devoted." Sadie didn't plan on letting her feelings slip out. She'd divulge her infatuation with Vince in due time. First, she'd have to admit her reemerging feelings to herself.

"You're beautiful, smart, and funny. You'll meet someone who appreciates you. I'm sure of it." Jill put her arm around Sadie's shoulder.

"Maybe I've already met him." She raised a shoulder. *Oops. Me and my big mouth.*

Millie strolled over and squeezed in between them. "It seems pretty intense over here."

"We were discussing how fortunate Jill is to have a dedicated boyfriend," Sadie said.

"Sadie is interested in someone from her past," Jill blurted. "It's that guy from your theater group, right?" She raised her voice. "I knew you were a little too eager to see his show. Didn't you have a thing for him in school? That's settled, we're going," Jill insisted.

Millie listened in and displayed a big smirk. "Your face is red, and it's not from the sun."

"Yes, I liked him, but no big deal. Vince is a great guy, and I'm ready this time around. Is that okay with you two?" She held back a grin. This new lease on life had taken on a whole new dimension.

"We're ecstatic." The two of them glanced at each other and giggled.

"Seriously, I think kismet has this one. How else

can you explain running into him?" Jill added.

Sadie wasn't about to argue. There was something to her friend's candid statement. There was no rational explanation why she'd run into someone out of her past so far away from home.

"Could be." Millie pursed her lips and nodded in agreement. "The water is so clear I can see the bottom perfectly." She peeled off her graphic, oversized tee.

Sadie lowered herself in the pool. "It's warm, yet cool enough to be refreshing." She splashed her arms and chest. "Come on in." She kicked her feet to stay afloat, feeling young and carefree. After a cold winter spent mostly indoors, heck, she'd skinny-dip if it was allowed. Her friends slowly sampled the water. After a few minutes, you'd have thought they were high school kids laughing and tossing around a beach ball.

"I can't wait to check out this man that's got you all excited. Oh, don't get me wrong, I'm happy for you. I just want to make sure he's good enough for you," Millie announced as she rested her arms over the side of the pool.

"I'm with you, Millie. Our girl deserves a prince."

"Thanks, you two." It was a comfort to have friends so devoted. Sadie knew how much her best buddies loved her and she loved them too. It was a gift to have such caring friends, even if they drove her nuts sometimes.

****

The three of them spent longer than expected at poolside, so they'd have to rush to grab a quick bite to eat before the show. "Who's in the mood for pizza?" Sadie asked as she pushed aside her outfits in the closet, looking for her turquoise dress.

"Sounds good to me." Jill stood in front of the mirror, checking her tan line.

"Me too." Millie plugged in her phone charger and sat on the bed.

"Great. That's about all we'll have time for. I think there's an Italian place in the food court." Sadie was the first to jump into the shower.

"I'm next," Jill insisted.

As soon as Sadie finished and came out, Jill made a dash into the bathroom. There was an outlet next to the mirrored dresser where Sadie plugged in the blow dryer. By the time she was halfway through with her hair, Jill shouted from behind the door. "Be right out, Millie." In a few minutes, garbed in a terry cloth robe, Jill parked herself next to Sadie.

"I'm finished with my hair." Sadie handed Jill the blow dryer, went over to the closet to grab her cosmetic bag, and went back in front of the mirror.

"You want to time me? Watch this." Millie jolted into the bathroom. In less than ten minutes she came out. "I'm used to getting in and out." She gave a cackle.

They'd set a record for quickest time getting ready for a night out. Sadie stopped in front of the mirror in the foyer. She fluffed her hair and took a closer look at her face.

"You look gorgeous. He won't be able to resist you." Jill picked up her purse from the bed.

"I'd say not. You're a knock-out," Millie insisted.

"Promise the teasing ends here." Sadie tried to keep a serious face. She opened the door, stepped aside, and held her arm out. "You first."

The girls filed out into the hallway. Sadie's hands trembled. Her nerves were on edge, and she rode the elevator with her eyes closed to concentrate on a few deep breathing exercises.

"Are you okay?" Jill gave her a side look.

"I'm better than ever. A little anxious, but in a good way."

****

After a stop at the pizzeria in the hotel, Sadie reapplied her peachy lip-gloss. Butterflies filled her stomach. It was as if she was back on the opening night of her theater debut. She closed her eyes and silently assured herself that she'd do all right.

Sadie couldn't wait to introduce her friends to Vince, but she didn't want the girls to push too hard. If her instinct was right, he had more than a casual friendship in mind. Her spicy thoughts kept coming, and she went with them, instead of stuffing her emotions like she did in the past. There was nothing wrong with a harmless little fantasy, was there?

Clenching the program for the show in her hand, she smiled as they headed to the theater upstairs.

"Let's hurry." Sadie motioned. The three of them picked up speed as their heels clanked on the stunning marble floors.

There was a line of people waiting to go inside. The cast members stood outside the double door entrance, greeting each person as they entered. The buzz of congratulatory words and smiling faces set the tone for the evening.

As Sadie quietly chatted with her friends, her gaze lingered on Vince. His full head of dark hair was styled for a red carpet event. The gleam in his gorgeous eyes left her whole body weak. Her throat parched, she took out a cough drop and popped it into her mouth. His wide, welcoming smile helped her racing heart slow down.

"I'm so glad you could make it, Sadie." He took her by surprise by offering a hug. "You look beautiful tonight."

Her new sheath dress had made a hit. "Thank you. You look great too. Break a leg." She gave him a big smile. "These are my friends, Jill and Millie." She turned and gave them a wink, hoping they'd fix their faces. They both gawked at Vince as if he were a male stripper. Sadie's fingers tingled as she tapped the lapel on his tailored black jacket. Even the most innocent touch sent her over the deep end.

"It's a pleasure to meet you, ladies." Vince reached out to shake their hands. "I arranged for front row seats."

He lightly touched Sadie's back as he guided them toward the usher, and it sent an electric surge through her body.

"I hope you enjoy the show. Please accept my invitation to a party in the Midnight Rooftop Bar after the show," Vince said.

Sadie found his hospitality along with his smile absolutely irresistible. He went out of his way to make a good impression. His thoughtfulness gave him brownie points for sure. As they made their way down the aisle, her legs shook. She'd been up on the stage next to him, and now she'd watch from the audience. Very different.

Jill dug her finger into Sadie's side. "We're going to that party." She did a little shimmy.

"I know. Stop, he's watching," Sadie whispered.

Millie leaned in close and said, "It looks like your

feelings are reciprocated."

Sadie couldn't help but gloat. First row center seats were perfect. Once they settled in, she stared at the curtain in anticipation of Vince's performance. The cameras and lighting were all set and ready to go. It put her in mind of the days when all she wanted was to be on the stage. The cameramen scattered around the front. The lights brightened. A man came out to help energize the audience, and then the curtain opened.

****

Vince took his bow and headed to the dressing area. His mind raced with things he would have done different, yet the audience's laughter and applause had been steady. With the woman he'd never forgotten in the audience, his energy soared and he'd done his best to make sure his performance was near flawless. He thought it was anyway. Now he'd have to wait for the feedback.

His leading lady had worked the stage like a pro, and he knew by the laughter out front, she'd hit the mark. Her delivery was on point. The supporting cast did a great job. It all magically fell together. The hard work, rehearsal after rehearsal, long hours, and commitment had all paid off. It was one of the highlights of his life. Hopefully, the network would decide to pick up the show.

The director congratulated the cast as they gathered off stage. After Vince did a quick change, he hurried to catch the girls out front.

Sadie made her way over to him with a big smile on her face. Vince's heart pranced as soon as she met his gaze.

"You were fantastic. I believe you have a hit on

your hands," she insisted.

"I have a good feeling too." He was still on a high from the show, and it kicked up a notch when he stood side by side with the sexy and gorgeous woman from his past. She took his breath away, and the night was still young.

Jill and Millie appeared and gave him a round of applause.

"You rocked it." Jill put her hand on his shoulder.

"I appreciate your support, ladies. Thank you." His attention switched to Sadie. "Can you make it to the party?" It was funny how his insides rattled as he waited for her reply. He'd performed in front of an audience with no problem, but around Sadie, he was putty in her hands.

"We're looking forward to it." Sadie's comment set him at ease. Vince shot a look over to the others.

"I'll be able to stay for a bit, but I have to get my beauty sleep," Jill said, then she gave Millie a nudge.

"Oh, umm…me too."

He winked, in tune with what they were up to. He'd come to know how intuitive girlfriends could be. It was like they had psychic abilities or something. He recalled when a woman he'd dated briefly had introduced him to her close-knit group of friends. They'd zeroed in on his inability to commit to the relationship from the start. She wasn't right for him, and his career goals came first. Sadie was here now, and he'd do whatever it took to win her heart.

In the elevator to the rooftop together, Sadie stood close. The sweet scent of her hair, along with her delicate perfume filled the small space, and it made him want her even more. An endorphin rush shot through his body, enhancing his senses. She embodied sexiness in a feminine, yet smart, classy way. It didn't seem like she had to work hard to look beautiful. Nature took care of that.

Vince held his breath as they approached the bar. After all, it was his first celebratory party. It was important to him to make a good impression on Sadie and her friends. Glittering white lights hung around the perimeter and a dangling crystal ball hung over the dance floor. Scattered tall, round tables, love seats with plush red cushions, and modern black wrought iron tables were in the center. Servers dressed in black vests carried trays of finger foods, and others served champagne. People seemed to be enjoying themselves already. By the sound of the laughter in the audience, the show had struck a chord. With a beautiful woman at his side, life couldn't get much better. All heads turned when Vince entered. A round of applause began, and he smiled and raised his hand to signal to go on with the fun. Out of the corner of his eye, he spotted his manager.

"I want you to meet someone," Vince said. "I wouldn't have gotten this role if it weren't for my manager." He motioned for Joey to join them.

Joey approached. He was a stout man with a thinning hairline. "You're a superstar, my man," Joey exclaimed. He shook Vince's hand with a firm grip.

"I'd like you to meet an old friend, Sadie Layne, and her friends, Millie and Jill." Vince's heart swelled with pride as he enjoyed his moment of fame.

"It's my pleasure, ladies." Joey cleared his throat and patted Vince on the back. He waved his hand to a young man with a tray of drinks, and the server approached. "I'd like to propose a toast." He handed them each a glass of champagne and took one for himself. "Everyone here is of drinking age, right?" he joked.

Vince appreciated his manager's hard work on his behalf, but he hoped Joey refrained from cracking a string of his usual corny one-liners. Not tonight.

"To a talented cast, hardworking crew, and a long run on primetime." Joey raised his glass in the air.

"To Vince, for much deserved happiness and continued success." Sadie sipped her champagne and offered him a poised smile.

It took restraint on his part to keep from reaching over and kissing her right there on the rooftop. Her eyes sparkled under the bright lights, and the evening breeze made her hair flow gently, which gave him a clear view of her beauty. His heart stood still. For a moment, it seemed as if they were alone in the world.

Jill spoke and broke the spell. "I think you have a hit, Vince. I enjoyed the show, and the audience seemed to feel the same." She moved close to Millie and slipped her arm through hers. "We have to get our rest. Thank you so much for inviting us. Sadie, I'm sure you want to stay a little longer. I'll keep a nightlight on in the room." One of the servers passed by carrying an empty tray, and she placed her glass on it.

Sadie remained quiet, and he was mesmerized as he kept his eyes on her. So far his plan was going smoothly. Just as he was about to sweep her into a spot where they could see the best view, the big guns approached.

"Great job tonight," Dick Mann, the producer, said. With a great reputation and a couple of Emmys behind him, Dick had an eye for a potential award winner. His boisterous laugh and large stature commanded the room.

"Thanks. Everyone fed off the energy in the room. I'd like you to meet a friend of mine, Sadie Layne."

"It's very nice to meet you. Are you an actress?" Dick asked.

Sadie shifted her position and fiddled with her watch. "No, I'm a drama teacher."

He nodded and smiled. "That's fantastic. Did you enjoy the show?"

"I did. I loved it." She caught Vince's gaze and put on an endearing grin.

"Good. I'm glad to hear that. Well, enjoy the festivities." The executive gave Vince a forceful pat on the back, and in moments, he moved on to the other cast members.

"Now, where was I?" Vince took Sadie by the hand and guided her to a quieter area. A large branch from a palm in the right position gave them a few minutes of privacy.

Sadie crossed her arms and shivered.

"Are you cold? It's chilly up here tonight, but the stars are shining for us." Vince slipped his arm around her.

"Maybe a little. I'm in awe of the view. This is such a gorgeous city." Sadie snuggled up close.

"It is. Just as I'm getting used to it, I'm flying home soon," he responded and wished they'd had more time.

"I'm here for the week." She wiggled away and stood directly in front of him. She parted her lips and put on a sultry stare. Sadie took hold of his heart.

48

"You look more stunning than ever tonight." Vince kept his voice low.

Then, he acted on impulse. He placed his hands on the sides of her face. When she responded with a smile, he couldn't resist another minute. His heart soared as he gazed down at her. Sadie uttered a soft moan as their lips met. She reached up and placed her arms around his neck, quivered slightly, and nestled up against him, as if she'd wanted him to kiss her all along. His knees weakened as he sampled the sweet peach lip-gloss on her soft, luscious lips.

As he savored each moment, his heart pounded in his ears. If he didn't break free, he wouldn't be able to stop himself. He was afraid to open his eyes to find it was all a dream. Vince tried to keep his cool as his breathing sped up like he'd run a marathon. His head spun with thoughts of making love to this amazing woman. Oh, how he wanted to show her how much she meant to him, but he'd wait. One thing he had learned from the way his father had treated his mother was to respect a woman. Sadie deserved so much more. Once their tender moment ended, he stood back, lost in her gaze.

"I'm crazy about you, Sadie. I always have been, but if I'm going too fast, please stop me." He spoke close to her ear. Vince ran his finger along her cheek and gently lifted her chin. "We met up again this many miles away from Jersey for a reason." He pushed a strand of her silky, blonde hair away from her beautiful eyes.

"You might have something there," she agreed. "Don't worry, I'll let you know if you get out of line."

She gave him a seductive stare and devilish smirk,

which was out of character for Sadie, but he liked it. She had always been warm and friendly, but not the kind of girl who'd make a first move. Although, she did mention how her cancer scare changed her views on life. Whatever the reason for exposing her sensual side, it was certainly working in his favor.

Vince dropped his arm to meet her waist and turned her to face the star-lit sky. A peace surrounded him as their bodies touched. He took a deep breath, all the time hoping he'd be able to leave early. When he snuck a quick look through the branches, he spotted Joey scanning the room.

"I'll be right back. Wait for me here," Vince said.

Sadie nodded and smiled. "I'm not going anywhere."

He ducked and weaved to get to his manager. Joey appeared next to the buffet, and he reached out and tapped his shoulder. "Hey, buddy."

Joey turned to face him, holding onto his plate.

"I have plans later, but I'll stop over and make an appearance to all the big wigs before I leave."

"I know what you're up to, and I don't blame you for one minute. If I had a babe like that, I'd do the same." He gave a devilish grin.

"Hold on. Sadie is an old friend and a wonderful person." On occasion, Vince had to remind Joey to mind his manners.

"I meant no harm. You know what I mean. Make the rounds and then get the hell out of here." Joey gave Vince a friendly shove.

Once he showed his face in all the circles on the rooftop, Vince hurried back to Sadie. "I'm sorry, I had to pull a few strings, but we're free to leave now," he announced.

"I didn't mind waiting. It gave me time to bask in the glory of this amazing city."

Sadie was not only talented, gorgeous, and sexy, but her sweet, understanding personality had captured his heart. She'd spent many hours reading lines and coaching him back in the day. She had a natural talent for teaching. Her passion for the theater came across loud and clear. His heart raced with the thought of being alone with her. He needed to get his act together and not push too hard. She wouldn't want a man who was too pushy.

Vince was relieved to be able to slip away with Sadie without the rest of the cast insisting he stay a little longer. At the elevator, he could relax and enjoy their time alone. The best of the evening was yet to come.

"I hope your friends won't be annoyed that I took you away from your after-party so soon." Her eyelashes fluttered, and her innocent flirtation made him want her more. One glass of champagne and he fell deeper under Sadie's spell.

He steadied himself. "Not at all. Half of them won't even remember the party. Anyway, how often do you run into someone as special as you after so many years?" In his heart knew every word of it was true. "Are you hungry?"

"Maybe a tiny bit. We stopped for a slice of pizza before the show. How about you?"

"I could go for a midnight snack. I have an idea. We could order room service and kick back in my suite. The night is still young, and this way we can catch up."

"I'd like that."

He didn't want Sadie to get the wrong idea. Sure, he desired nothing more than to be alone with her, however, if she wanted to talk, he'd talk all night. Anything to be close to her.

Vince had an inkling when she had first approached him in the lobby, and by the more than flirtatious tone in her voice, that he'd finally have a chance with his former classmate. She'd grown into a mature woman, and he had a feeling Sadie knew all too well what she wanted. So he'd let her lead the way. He'd take things slow until he got a sign. One thing he wanted to make clear was that he didn't want a one-night stand. He wanted to build something that would last. No matter what was going on in his career, he had time for Sadie. They'd make it work, somehow. He'd grab this second chance and never let go.

Chapter 3

Vince's suite was top of the line. The minute she stepped inside, Sadie felt like she'd marched onto a set of *Lifestyles of the Rich and Famous*, a show her mother used to watch when she was a kid. She was impressed, to say the least. He'd hit the big time. It was three times the size of her room, with a beautifully designed mirror on the largest wall, a king-sized bed dressed in a clean white, red, and beige color scheme, a seating area adorned with elegant burgundy and gold upholstery, a separate room with a desk, and a huge marble bath. She stole a better peek at the bathroom, and the tub was big enough to swim in. She gasped when she saw the size of the huge rain shower with glass doors. It could fit the whole neighborhood. The upgraded space suited her just fine.

He double-checked the lock on the door, went over to the dresser, and picked up a leather version of the room service menu. A round table was already set up by the floor-to-ceiling windows. An elegant white tablecloth and white china with gold edging was waiting for them.

"So, this is how the other half lives?" Sadie said.

"Nice, right?" He moved over to the wall of windows and pushed the silky, gold drapes all the way back.

"How did they know to set the table up?"

"It was done late this afternoon. The manager had anticipated I might bring the party up here. The staff goes out of their way for the guests."

"Oh, really?" she teased. She sauntered around the room, amazed at the details.

"It's not what you think," Vince insisted, his eyes fixed on her as she moved over to the window.

"Sure." She held back a smirk. "No, really, I'm impressed. You seem to be doing well in life."

Vince stood next to the bar and took out a bottle of Zinfandel from the refrigerator. "Would you like a glass of the finest?" He held the bottle up.

"Yes, I'd love one."

With glasses, a corkscrew, and the bottle in hand, he headed to the table in front of the love seat and placed them down. "The budget for the show paid for this. Believe me, I'm getting by, but I can't afford this. Not yet anyway. One day. Right now, I rent a tiny space back home in a boarding house a block from the beach." He popped the cork and poured a couple of glasses, then Sadie joined him. They both sat.

"Not bad. I remember how much you love the water."

"You do?"

He gave her the cutest smile that made her shiver. It was as if she'd told him the secret to the universe. Vince put the menu on the bed. He reached for her, gently took hold of her shoulders, and pulled her close. This time, the kiss was hot and heavy. His fingers trailed along her back, and each stroke made her temperature rise. The sound of her heart beating pounded in her ears as she melted into his strong arms. *Who needs food?*

"I didn't bring you up here to seduce you," he said, his tone deep, yet low.

"I know, Vince. It's been a long time coming." Sadie sighed as she held his gaze. She wasn't going to miss out on the opportunity to be with Vince. Life was far too short. She had first-hand experience. She was one of the lucky ones. A few of the friends she'd made in the oncologist office weren't as fortunate. They'd lost their battle.

He rested his hand on her thigh. "Do you mean it? If you'd rather grab something in the food court, I'd go along with you."

"I'm fine. I've changed my mind about eating."

"It's funny, now that you mention it, so have I. All of the excitement from the show and then being with you. I'm one privileged man." He cradled her face in his hands and moved up close. His lips found hers and locked into an embrace. She uttered a soft moan.

Her decision to push fear aside, along with the gift of a full recovery, gave Sadie the green light to move forward. She smiled and raised her hand to Vince's chest and massaged it, going in circles, moving close enough to feel his warm breath on her face. Every stroke was smooth and unplanned, as if her heart had taken over and led the way. Vince's breathing sped up as he slowly unbuttoned the top of his shirt. She went with raw instinct coupled with intense desire. She hadn't unleashed her sensual side like this before, and now, alone in his room, she wanted nothing more than to make love to the man she'd let get away so very long ago.

Even though it was a much-needed step, the change in behavior shocked even her. Who would have thought the prim and proper teacher was capable of such behavior? Not that Vince wasn't desirable, but she was moving as fast as a floozy. It was as if they'd entered a time machine and were zapped to where they'd left off. The comfort and familiarity of their connection had never shattered. It had intensified into something more, stronger and deeper on every level. Words weren't needed. She pulled back for a second, her head buzzing.

"Are you okay?" He gave a slight frown.

"I'm wonderful," she happily replied.

How on earth was she supposed to explain spending the night out to her friends? Her heart told her to stay with Vince. It wasn't as if they'd just met. Some of the students in the workshop had told her he'd had the hots for her, nevertheless, she'd insisted it was platonic. It took honesty on her part to admit she'd had a strong physical attraction to him. All these years her fairy-tale romance was right in front of her eyes, and she had looked past it to put her acting career first. Her whole world had revolved around the theater. How could she have lied to herself for so long? If she'd known her path would divert into a different direction, she might have done things differently. At the time, her goals had come before any form of romance. No more. Not this time. She was going for it. *Full speed ahead, girl. So long regrets.*

"You have no idea how much I want you, and I always have. You're the most gorgeous woman I've ever seen. There is no other woman who can compare to you, Sadie."

He trailed his tongue along her cheek and nibbled at her neck. Chills ran rampant through her body. Each gentle touch of his strong fingers along the inside of her thigh getting higher and higher. Sadie's arousal escalated, and she wanted nothing more than to rip his clothes off. He made his way back up to her mouth, and she parted her lips to welcome his tongue. His passionate kiss intensified her longing to have all of him.

"I want you too," she whispered softly.

Thank goodness the surgeon was one of the best, and she barely had a scar. Not that Vince would mind. She'd seen his sensitive and caring side when they used to do lawn work for the elderly people in town. He was a true gentleman. Sadie snuggled up close.

"I'm all yours." He scooped her up in his arms, took her over to the bed, and gently lowered her.

She ran her fingers over the luxurious, soft bedspread and up to an oversized, satin, crimson red throw pillow. It was like touching a fluffy cloud. "Everything in this room is perfect."

"Not as perfect as you." He stood in front of her, his gaze fixed on her.

Vince lifted her dress, and she wiggled out of it, warmth traveling in between her legs. He shed his shirt and hurried to take off his pants. He'd always turned her on and she couldn't wait to show him how much. A light tan enhanced his muscular physique. When she gently raked her fingers along his chest, his skin sizzled under her fingertips.

"Is it okay?" he asked as he lightly brushed his tongue over her breasts.

"Yes, go ahead. I'm better than ever," Sadie insisted.

He moved his hand across her back, unclasping her bra and removing it. Vince encircling her nipples with the tip of his tongue. He brushed his finger across each, making them swell in size. When he lowered his head and kissed her breasts, Vince's gentle approach transported Sadie to a pleasure zone she'd never thought possible. She arched her back, silently begging him to explore every inch of her body, soft moans hard to contain. Vince got on his knees, his lips traveling across her stomach as light as a butterfly. He playfully edged his fingers under the elastic on her bikinis until they were on the floor. Sadie's hot spot moistened and pulsated with desire.

"You're driving me wild, baby." His shaft was up against her leg, throbbing and growing in size as she tempted him with each movement.

"You're what I want." She swept her tongue across her dry lips. Pent-up passion drove her to finally show Vince how much she'd always adored him. Denial was no longer in control. Sadie reached for his waist, pulling him with an urgency, her desire mounting.

"Here I am." Vince moved on top of her, his warm body finally entangled with hers.

"I can't wait any longer." The time had come to give herself to her long-lost love. She grabbed onto his shoulders, digging her fingers into his skin. The soft sheets caressed her bare buttocks.

"You have no idea how much I've always wanted you," Vince whispered in her ear.

Sadie wrapped her legs tightly around him. His hair matted across his face. This man brought out a side of her she hadn't shown anyone she had ever dated. Only in her wildest daydreams did she let her body make all the decisions. Vince entered her, and she lifted her hips.

"Oh, Vince. Oh…Oh!" She took hold of his

buttocks.

"How on earth am I going to ever let you go? You're a goddess, and I'm your slave." He lifted his chest and stared deep into her eyes. His cheeks took on a flush, while tiny beads formed on his forehead. "Oh, baby. You are amazing," Vince said, his tone hoarse.

"So are you," she whispered.

"You're driving me out of my mind."

He placed his mouth on hers, his tongue traveling deep, searching. Shivers zipped down her spine. Each movement of his hips forced him deeper inside of her. The bed vibrated beneath them. Moist and pulsating, her hot spot was on fire.

"I'm sorry. It's just that you feel so good." His movements hastened and his breathing was rapid. Vince cried out, "Oh, baby! Baby!

Their bodies united with a fierce desperation. The bed rattled against the wall and the pillow dropped to the floor. "Don't stop. Oh, oh!" She gripped onto his buttocks and rode along with his lead. Her heart thumped next to his, and she didn't care if the whole world heard them. The room narrowed, and Sadie closed her eyes, her body as light as a feather.

Vince trembled as he held her tight, his face buried in her neck. Her head spun as she caught her breath. Wrapped in his arms, lying skin to skin, her entire body quivered. She never wanted the night to end. If this was what she'd been missing, she'd never hold back her feelings again.

They eventually fell asleep in each other's arms. Vince snored so loud it woke her, and she turned to check the time. If she didn't hurry and text the girls, they'd put a missing person report out on her by the morning. She held her breath and tried not to wake him by slowly edging over the side of the bed. Luckily, her purse was nearby, and she snatched it up in a hurry. She quietly got up and tiptoed to the bathroom and closed the door, leaving it cracked. Thank goodness for the soothing sound of the air conditioning. Vince never flinched.

She quickly texted Millie and Jill that she was still with Vince and she would be back in the morning. Jill was a light sleeper. She'd observed how she checked her cellphone habitually and always heard the signal.

Within minutes she got a return text.

You little run around. Have fun. Bless your heart.

Sadie put her hand to her mouth to keep from laughing. After a few more minutes in the bathroom, she snuck back and slipped into bed. She wasn't used to running through the night naked. Her clean bill of health had opened the door to a new lease on life, and it was long overdue.

Vince looked adorable curled up in bed with his eyes closed. She slid over close enough to feel the heat from his body, then slowly placed her leg over his. Listening to Vince breathe was like music to her ears. The feeling of contentment was unfamiliar, but she welcomed it.

In the morning, Vince's phone buzzed and it startled her. She jumped up, dazed, and for a moment, she had to concentrate to remember she'd let her friends know she was sleeping out. He turned to face her and gently moved her hair away from her eyes.

"I'm sorry my manager called so early. I've got an appointment to do an interview for a celebrity news show this morning. I'd almost forgotten about it." He twisted his lips into a pout. "Will you be upset if I have to jump in the shower without making love to you again?"

"So, I slept with a celebrity? I think I'll be fine," she assured him.

"Well, I don't know. You're a hot mama." He gave a sly grin.

"I'm going to get you." Sadie tickled him until he begged her to stop. He squirmed around on the bed and let out a hearty laugh. "Say you're sorry or I'll keep going." She tried to keep a straight face. It was fun to be able to be herself with a man. She'd read that laughter was a great way to keep a relationship alive. In the back of her mind, she had questions. Was last night the start of something serious or simply friends who let the bright lights and excitement of LA cloud their senses?

"I'm so sorry." He gently broke free and hurried into the bathroom. "I'll be quick. Please wait for me."

"I'll close my eyes for a few more minutes," she shouted across the room. Memories of their romantic evening helped her drift back to sleep.

"Sleepyhead, wake up."

Sadie opened her eyes to find Vince dressed to kill.

"That was quick," she said.

"I don't waste any time."

"You sure don't." She sat up and reached for her clothes from the bedside chair. She put on her bra and panties.

Vince sat alongside of her and caressed her thigh, sending a wave of heat to her belly. "Last night was unreal. Thank you for staying the night. You're unbelievable."

Sadie turned her head and gently planted her mouth on his. It was as natural as breathing to be with Vince. Crazy, but in a good way. He nibbled on her bottom lip, his arms tight around her back.

"I'm having second thoughts about leaving you." He stared deep into her eyes and hesitated as his gaze dipped down to the floor. "I have to run or I'll be late. I can grab coffee downstairs. Do you want me to order breakfast for you?"

"No thanks. I'm good." Her heart sunk as she settled back on the bed and curled up into a fetal position. Sadie was disappointed that they couldn't spend the morning together.

A cold chill in the room was different than the heat of the night. Reality had set in, and she knew that a teacher and an up-and-coming actor might be a mismatch. His career should come first. Sadie shook her head and tried to put a halt to her negative thoughts. After a dreamy night filled with passion, a quick goodbye wasn't what she'd hoped for.

Vince headed to the door and then stopped short. He suddenly turned around. "I've got to be out of my mind." He hastened back to Sadie and sat on the edge of the bed. "There's plenty of time before the interview. I'll break my obsessive habit of being an hour early for everything. I'm ordering breakfast for two."

"I'd love coffee with cream and sugar." Sadie smiled and shimmied her hips around before she sat back up.

"Actually, I remember how you like your coffee. We used to need plenty of Joe when we stayed at the playhouse to rehearse."

"That's right. We guzzled the boxed coffee from

the donut shop like it was going out of style." She laughed aloud.

"We did have some great times. You better get into the bathroom to get dressed. They're pretty quick here, and I wouldn't want the servers gawking at you under the covers." He stood.

"No, me either. I'm going, but first things first." Sadie hopped out of bed, still half-naked, and cuddled up against his chest. She stood on her toes to reach his lips.

"Wow, now where am I supposed to go?" He remained in one spot as he scratched his head.

"Now you can place the order." She danced all the way into the bathroom.

Vince gave a whistle.

"Very funny." Sadie giggled as she closed the door.

By the time she finished dressing, breakfast had arrived and the table was adorned with an arrangement of pink, purple, and white fresh flowers in a crystal vase. "How beautiful."

"Not as beautiful as you." He pulled out her chair and she sat.

Sadie's head was in the clouds as she poured cream and added two packets of sugar to her morning brew. She reached over, grabbed a piece of cinnamon toast, and spread a dab of butter on it. Lifting her mug, she inhaled the robust aroma of the coffee, then took a sip. She ate her toast and finished her coffee.

"What a wonderful place to have breakfast." She sighed and stared out at the view of the Hollywood sign. "This is magnificent. I never want to leave."

"I hear you. One could get used to this," Vince

agreed. He placed his elbow on the table and rested his hand on the side of his face as he gazed at her.

"What's wrong?"

"Oh, not a thing. I was thinking how sexy you look in the morning."

Things couldn't get much better. Sadie poured another cup of coffee. "Thanks for ordering room service. I should get going." She sighed, wanting nothing more than to seduce him back into bed.

"Is something bothering you? That was a heavy sigh." Vince reached out to touch her hand.

"I was thinking about the barrage of questions I'm about to face. Just preparing myself." She offered a hesitant smile and fiddled with a sugar packet. "I don't want to hold my friends up. We have plans. I suppose it's time to get to the beach and later our anticipated shopping spree." She had managed to tuck a few bucks away to splurge if she spotted something she absolutely had to have.

"I'm sure your friends want you to be happy. And besides, if running into one another is not fate, I don't know what is."

His analogy was convincing. "Yeah, but…"

He lifted one shoulder. "They both winked at me when they left the party early." Vince gave her an assuring grin. "Believe me, they knew before you did. I'm grateful for their help." He stood and glanced at his watch "We better get going."

Sadie respected the fact that he wanted to be early for the interview. She appreciated his effort to spend a little more time together.

Vince stepped over to her side of the table. Sadie stood, and he cradled her in his arms. He lightly brushed his lips across her cheek. His stubble made her face tingle. She was still reluctant to explain why she spent the night with Vince to her friends. There were so many things to consider. Daylight brought the real world into play.

"I'll leave with you. This way you can lock up."

"Thanks for understanding," Vince said.

Sadie grabbed her bag and joined him at the door. "Here's my number." She handed Vince her card.

"I'll call you. Have fun today. LA is a great city."

As she watched him get into the elevator, Sadie got a burst of energy, and she decided to take the stairs one floor down to her room. She needed time to think about all that had changed in such a short time. When she made a decision to stop being so conservative and take more chances, she never imagined things would happen so fast.

She slipped the card in the door and entered her room, expecting to find Millie and Jill inside. Housekeeping must have already been there. She checked the bathroom and it was spotless. The girls probably ran down to get a latte. Sadie shed her clothes and jumped into the shower.

The warm water filtering down her spine put her in a relaxed and content place. The green tea body wash the hotel supplied was soothing and aromatic. When she finished, she went over to the closet and picked out a white pair of capris with a red, sleeveless top and white, strappy sandals. With a touch of makeup, a pair of diamond stud earrings, and a straw bag, she was out the door.

While Sadie waited for the elevator, she dialed Millie's number. "Hey, girlfriend. I'm on my way down. Are you in the coffee shop?"

"We'll be waiting near the door," Millie said, then blabbed about the list of places to visit.

She found Jill and Millie sprawled out on an orange leather love seat with yellow throw pillows, and they waved her over.

"What's on the agenda?" Sadie asked. "How about a walk on the beach and then on to Rodeo Drive for lunch?" A surge of adrenaline shot through her body. How wonderful to be on an exciting adventure, cancer free, and with romance on the back burner.

"I hope you don't think you're getting off the hook without details." Jill stood and put her arm around her friend's shoulder. They headed outside.

Sadie's heart thumped. Where to begin? Now, she'd have to admit to her friends and to herself why the relationship with Vince might not work. "Come on." Sadie turned to signal to Millie.

Millie got up and caught up to them. "Let's catch a cab, and then you can tell us all about it on the beach," she suggested.

The west coast sky didn't have a cloud in sight and the sun gleamed, but it wasn't a scorcher. The branches of a pretty palm outside of the hotel swayed as a gust of wind swept by, yet the sky kept its bright shade of blue. It was certainly a bonus day.

"It's an ideal day for sight-seeing." She held her shoulders back, all the time her night of passion rewinding in her head.

****

The cab service that a friendly woman at the front desk had suggested got them to Santa Monica Pier in less than thirty minutes.

"I love The Jersey Shore, but the water here is gorgeous." Sadie couldn't believe she was trekking along the beach in Santa Monica, California, with her feet in the crystal blue water and her toes sinking into the wet sand. Between the palm trees, the vintage pier, and the view of the stately hotels along the beach, she didn't know if she'd ever want to go home.

Jill took out her camera and snapped pictures of the old-fashioned pier. "Smile."

Sadie struck a pose with a hand on her hip, her hair tousled from the warm ocean breeze. Millie got close and Jill snapped a photo of the two of them.

"Let me have the camera. I'll take one of you," Sadie insisted.

A young couple strolled by hand and hand and they offered to take a picture of all of them.

"This one is going into a frame." Sadie held the camera up to let Jill and Millie take a peek.

After an hour of fun in the sun and exploring the pier, it was time for lunch. Sadie gathered her things and folded her beach towel. "Let's check out the shopping area like we'd planned. I already called the cab."

"Sounds good to me," Jill agreed.

"Me too," Millie chimed in. "I can't wait to hear about your night with Vince."

"I was hoping you both forgot about it, but I guess not." She took a long, deep breath.

They both pouted and begged like little kids until Sadie gave in.

"Don't worry. I'll tell you most of what happened." A wave of heat rushed over her cheeks. She knew they cared about her well-being and wanted her to be happy.

Why was it so difficult to talk about Vince?

****

After strolling into an eclectic shop in the third street promenade, they each purchased a silver balance bracelet with a different inspirational quote on each.

"Let's get a massage. This looks like a nice clean place," Jill shouted.

Since Sadie wanted to be spontaneous, she agreed and nodded to Millie.

"Let's do it," Millie responded.

In the backroom with patchouli candles and the sound of the ocean in the backdrop, they got pampered, and Sadie dozed off with thoughts of Vince prancing around her head.

Relaxed and raring to go, they paid the bill and continued down the boardwalk like carefree hippies.

"That was worth every penny. I feel like a new person." Sadie smiled. A place with an outside seating area caught her attention. "We're having so much fun we forgot lunch. Late is better than none." Sadie pointed to the eatery. "What do you say?"

"Looks great, and smells good too," Jill said.

"I'm in. The aroma floating our way convinced me." Millie kept up with them.

Under a sun-filled sky, the scent of garlic and a fired-up grill led them to the open courtyard. An oversized, dark green awning hovered over a large area with round tables and elegant white linen tablecloths. Palms in huge planters sat in the corners.

"I wonder how the margaritas are." Once they were seated, Jill opened her menu.

"Sangria may be better for the daytime." Sadie adjusted her chair.

"You might be right." Jill grinned.

A young man wearing a red shirt monogrammed with the name of the eatery and a pair of black pants offered a pleasant greeting, took their orders, and returned with a basket of warm bread. He poured them each a glass of wine.

"Wine in the afternoon is wonderful." Jill raised her glass, twirled it a few times, and then took a sip.

"I think I see Brad and Angelina," Sadie squeaked.

Jill craned her neck. "I almost believed you."

"I'm sorry. I couldn't resist."

"How was it?" Jill buttered a roll.

"How was what?" She knew as soon as the food arrived, the drilling would begin.

"The sex with Vince. What do you think?" Her lips curled up in a grin.

"It was fantastic. Are you both happy now?" She held her breath and waited, her cheeks sizzling, embarrassed to admit how quickly they'd jumped into bed together.

"I didn't say a word," Millie barked.

"I'm sorry, you're right. I can't wait to hit the shops."

"A bit secretive, aren't we?" Jill returned as she crinkled up her nose.

"I'm not. Thanks for giving us time together, both of you. He noticed how you made a quick exit from the party and appreciated it. You know he's had a thing for me since the days in the theater group."

"We knew that, and we know you had it bad for him. Even though you won't admit it."

"What makes you think that?"

"We remember the story about the kiss in your

performance. You must have told us about it a zillion times. Who could forget?" The girls chuckled.

"You remember? I had forgotten all about it." *Who am I fooling?*

"If you and Vince make beautiful music together, go for it. That's my advice. I think he's a living doll, and he's a great performer. I laughed my ass off last night." Jill took another sip of wine.

"He is talented." Sadie's voice cracked as she played with her napkin. How was she going to deal with being with a man who lived the life that she always dreamed of? A constant reminder of her deepest regrets wasn't what she'd planned for. Although, when he held her close, nothing else mattered.

"You don't have to convince us, but it sounds like you need some convincing. How can we help?" Millie questioned.

"I know how wonderful Vince is. I'm going to see him again and go from there. It's a big change for me, and a huge step in the right direction." Sadie wasn't going to decide her future while she was on vacation. It was one night with an old friend. It was time to turn off the overthinking and simply have fun.

"I'm having whatever she's having for dessert." Jill nodded toward a mound of whipped cream with a strawberry topping and a ganache drizzle. "Sinful is my middle name."

"I'm with you. Later we can go to the hotel gym." Sadie gave a wide grin and a snort. "Don't let me forget to pick up my perfume. It will drive Vince wild."

****

At the small, brightly lit studio in downtown LA, a pretty, young, blonde-haired reporter wearing a vibrant blue, short dress sat across from Vince and asked him detailed questions about the pilot show and his next project. All he could think about was Sadie. He pushed the thoughts aside. How often did someone have a chance to appear on a top-rated show? His palms became sweaty and his throat tightened. The heat from the lights and the temperature in the room made his mouth dry.

During a break, he stood at the window, stared out at the amazing city, and wolfed down a bottle of water. Vince realized he needed to straighten up his act and focus or he'd mess up any chance of getting invited back for another spotlight.

By the second half of the show, he was able to concentrate and his words flowed. The journalist's warm and friendly approach eventually helped set him at ease. When he finally gathered his thoughts and relaxed, the words came easy. He'd worked too hard to mess up this chance at taking his career to the next level. He felt it in his bones—his breakout role was coming.

"Thank you for a great interview, Vince." She stood and graciously shook his hand.

"It was my pleasure. Thank you."

"I'm looking forward to seeing your debut." She smiled. "I'll see you out."

"I appreciate it."

Once he got inside the backseat of the sleek, black Mercedes Benz that the studio had arranged for his interview, he scanned his messages. A text from his mother made his stomach twist and turn into knots. His parents were working things out, yet he had his doubts about a reconciliation. How many chances are one too many? Vince gave a long sigh. Maybe it was time to lighten up. His own life was far from perfect.

Never give up and keep going until you make it. That's what Joey, his manager, always told him. Going out to eat was a luxury with his tight budget. With rent, utilities, the cellphone bill, and car insurance, he made it a habit to stock up on sale items at the grocery store to keep going. Sadie deserved so much more than a man with high hopes and empty pockets. He gritted his teeth, determined to find a way to make it work.

Chapter 4

When Vince arrived at the hotel the chauffeur parked and opened the door for him. First class treatment was great.

Vince stepped out, relieved to have one more thing checked off his busy schedule. "Thank you. I appreciate it." He gave a quick nod as the driver got back into the car.

He gazed up at the amazingly clear sky, inhaled the fresh air, and wished he was able to extend his trip a few days. He must have checked his phone every minute during the ride. Vince had hoped to hear from Sadie. He missed her already. Although, she was technically on a girls' trip, and she might be busy having a great time. *Don't be selfish*, he told himself. Hopefully, she missed him a little too. There wasn't a moment to waste. One night with Sadie had made him realize what he'd been waiting for most of his adult life.

Why was he still feeling as uncertain as a high school student? He didn't want to come across as demanding, but he had to see Sadie again. His neck muscles stiffened, and as he stretched, he took a slow, cleansing breath. Not only was he anxious about the possibility of his pilot being rejected, he didn't want Sadie to think what they'd shared was a one-night stand. Sadie probably didn't have time for a serious relationship. She had so much going on in her life already.

He twisted his mouth to one side, took his phone out of his pocket, and checked his messages. Sadie was difficult to read. The playful way she'd made the first move and the way she didn't ask if he was going to call wasn't what he'd expected. It only made him want her more. She was as elusive as a butterfly.

He might be overthinking. What else was new? In the old days, he'd ride his bike to the playhouse, and he knew Sadie had a car. His old insecurities about being from the wrong side of town snuck up on him. He'd been escorted to an interview in the backseat of a Mercedes Benz. So, why was he still feeling as if he was back in high school?

He removed his shades, stuck them into his pocket, and went inside the hotel. He'd call Sadie tonight if he didn't hear from her first. It would be great if she had a free moment to squeeze him in. Vince tried to accept it for what it was—a night of passion with a woman from his past. That was what it was. Or was it?

Back in his room, he marched over to the wet bar and took out a bottle of water, opened it, and drank half of it. A cold brew was what he really could go for, but he had to resist. If he wanted to keep his body in shape, he'd refrain.

His stomach churned whenever he thought about what he'd missed out on by not pursuing Sadie in the past. She might have said yes. He'd never know, so he decided to read over a script for a made-for-TV movie his manager had thrown his way. The movie wasn't a definite, just a maybe. At least he had a variety of projects to fall back on.

It was about time he quit stalling and called his

mom to let her know how the show went. His biggest concern was how difficult it was for her since the separation. He admired how she'd gone back to school to become a nurse after his father's drinking had caused him to lose job after job. Vince had faith she'd be able to take care of herself. Her caregiving nature was perfectly suited for nursing. Thank goodness she didn't depend on him for financial help. Regret about not having a steady nine-to-five came in waves, however he'd always managed to rationalize his decision to keep his dream alive. He didn't know how he was going to take Sadie to nice places and show her the best of life. He exhaled. All in due time.

He picked up his phone to make the call. "Hey, Mom. How are you?" he said when she answered. He pulled out the desk chair, sat, and stared out the window.

"Oh, hi. I was hoping you'd call." Her upbeat, cheery tone helped to lessen some of his worries. "I did three twelve-hour shifts in a row this week. Glad it's over."

"You're amazing."

"I do what I have to do, but thanks. How did the pilot go? I said a prayer that you'd be great."

"I think we did what we set out to do—entertain and make people laugh. The audience went wild over it. I'm still waiting to hear about the scores. You'll never guess who I ran into in the hotel lobby." He stood and began to pace in anticipation of his announcement. His mother already knew Sadie from their theater days.

"Who? Are you going to tell me or keep me hanging?" she said.

"Do you remember Sadie Layne from my theater

group?"

"Oh, of course. You were crazy about her," she replied in a high-pitched voice. "Sadie was a lovely person and a wonderful actress. "Has she moved to LA?"

"No, she still lives in town. She's a drama teacher at the high school. It's strange how we haven't crossed paths much. I guess it's because we travel in such different circles now." He shrugged and continued pacing, his doubts about their relationship multiplying.

"That's nice, but she was set on being in the theater. I wonder what changed her mind."

"Who knows? She seems to enjoy what she's doing. I may be jumping the gun, but we got together, and I think we're going to see each other again. Maybe we'll pick it up when we get home. We'll see." He stopped a minute and stared out at the spectacular view, not wanting to face the fact that he'd never be able to afford a relationship until things picked up. They weren't kids anymore, and he'd feel like a failure asking Sadie to stay in and watch television. He began to see the veracity of timing.

"Oh, that would be fabulous. You have to bring her to the house for dinner. You two make a great couple."

"I will, Mom. Get some rest. I'll call you again before I leave."

"Okay. I hope you enjoy the rest of your stay. Talk to you soon."

Vince was pleased she had only good things to say about Sadie. He recalled that on the last night of their show, his mother and Sadie's had sat next to one another in the audience. He swore he heard them cheering all the way up on the stage. Ms. Layne was the one who encouraged his mother to go to nursing school. He looked forward to making new memories together.

His stomach growled. After a quick shower, he would run out to get something at the food court. He hadn't eaten since breakfast and he'd only had time to grab a protein bar. No wonder he was exhausted. The eucalyptus-scented body wash he bought in a shop in the hotel was supposed to be invigorating. He'd give it a try. The rain shower was just what he needed.

Once he lathered up, he let the water trickle down over his body. His mind wandered to the way Sadie ran her hand up and down his chest as she cuddled next to him. This magnificent woman had taken hold of his heart. Vince rinsed his hair, then he jumped out, toweled off, and got dressed. Jeans and a white t-shirt were the easiest. He'd only be out for a few minutes. For the rest of the night, he'd catch up on reading a few things his agent had given him.

He decided to go to his favorite place. Why play with perfection? This time he'd try a grilled chicken sandwich with a salad and a side of seasoned sweet potato fries.

He picked up his order from the counter and as he was about to leave, he decided to grab a bag of natural chocolate chip cookies and a container of milk. As he started back to his room, a few people in the lobby looked his way and whispered to one another. They must have recognized him from the pilot or maybe one of his commercials. It was nice to get a nod and a smile from strangers. As long as they enjoyed his work and he made them laugh, it was all worth it.

A few doors down from the restaurant, he stopped to check out the window in a jewelry shop. Diamond rings as bright as the sun were lined up in the front display. He glanced at them, and for a splint second, he envisioned putting one on Sadie's finger. He shook his head, laughed at himself, and tried to get a grip. *I'm a hopeless romantic with big dreams and empty pockets.* It wasn't the right time in his life to be thinking of such a thing. His friends were all in committed relationships. It was the time men his age thought about family, love, a house, and things like that. Strange how he didn't think about it until he held Sadie in his arms.

He started toward the elevators. The doors opened and Vince was pleasantly surprised when Sadie stepped out.

"Hi, Vince. What are you up to?" She offered him a perky smile.

"I was just thinking about calling you."

His heart danced in his chest. He pictured her wrapped in his arms and he had to fight the urge to plant a kiss on her luscious lips. He wasn't sure how she felt or what she had in mind about what had happened between them.

"Where are your friends?" he asked.

"They're getting ready. We're going to a popular restaurant for dinner. I came down for a bottle of Tylenol." She held up the bag with the medication and gave it a quick shake. "I took my last one on the plane." Sadie squinted and rubbed her forehead.

"Are you okay?"

"Too long in the sun and too much shopping. Add a lack of sleep to the mix." She put on a grin.

It wasn't his motive to detain her, but boy did she looked alluring in a pair of pink ankle-length pants and a sleeveless, floral top. A stylish white jacket finished off her look, and he couldn't take his eyes off her. "You look wonderful. I'd never guess you had a headache."

"After being in front of a class of teenagers, you learn how to hide it and cope." Sadie flipped her hand around and lifted a shoulder.

"You always were good at adapting to a situation." He got a whiff of her perfume as she brushed him with her arm and his head spun. "Do you remember the time we had to change costumes in between scenes and your zipper broke? You taped it closed, and it worked."

"I can't believe you remember that. What a crazy night." Sadie gave a sweet little giggle.

He moved aside and guided her to follow. "I don't want to block the entrance. Do you have plans later tonight?"

Sadie took a step closer. "We have plans for dinner."

She parted her lips, displaying the cutest expression. It made him want to sweep her up and carry her upstairs. The way her eyes glistened tantalized him to the core. She knew how to reel him in, and he was an easy catch. For her anyway. There was an honesty about Sadie that he'd always admired. She embodied the word integrity. He'd be proud to call her his girlfriend, if she'd have him.

"I'll be up late reading a few scripts. Do you want to come over when you get back?" He held his breath as his blood rushed to his head.

"I was thinking about it. I could pop over."

"Great! I'll be waiting. Tell the girls I said hello, and have a good time."

"I'll tell them. Thank you. When we get home, you can come to my house. I'll cook." She turned to push the button on the elevator.

"I'd like that."

They got inside together. After a short ride, Sadie got out on her floor. "I'll see you tonight."

He exhaled and mouthed a big *yes*. How did he get so lucky?

He wouldn't be able to invite her over to his place anytime soon. It wasn't a place you'd take a woman like Sadie. It was old, musty, cluttered with books, newspaper clippings, and mismatched furniture. A tiny studio and a bath, at his age, was embarrassing. His stomach tightened at the mere thought of her seeing where he lived. If he got a steady job, the first thing he would do was move to a bigger place. A steady job, besides waiting tables on weekends and modeling gigs, was long overdue.

The countdown had begun until he saw her again. He hurried up to his room, went over to the table, and opened the bag of food. The savory aroma made his mouth water. He dug in and finished it in minutes, saving the bag of cookies to share later with Sadie.

With a script in his hands, he plopped on the bed, kicked his shoes off, and arranged the pillows to be more comfortable. He'd promised Joey he'd read over a copy of the made-for-television movie. A long shot for sure. He'd had a busy couple of days. The pilot, a night with Sadie, an interview, and now another great night ahead of him. Less than halfway through the read, he couldn't keep his eyes open, and before long he dozed off.

****

After a delicious three-course dinner at an Italian restaurant in Beverly Hills, Sadie insisted that they order cappuccinos and dessert. Jill and Millie didn't put up much of a fight.

Sadie sat up straight and proudly announced, "I dieted for this trip."

"You've got a great figure, Sadie." Millie took a spoonful of her crème brûlée.

"Thanks. I cut down to be able to indulge."

"I feel like all eyes were on us tonight." Jill sampled a rich chocolate cake with ganache icing. She hunched over and whispered, "Did you notice how many people were staring at us? We must look like celebrities."

"I don't think so," Sadie replied. "Jill's imagination is over-the-top. She should have been the actress. We were lucky to get reservations in a place where the A-list stars are known to hang out."

The décor was modern and elegant, with gold and browns, leather booths, dark wood tables, vintage gold wall scones, and a huge bar with limestone granite. Throughout the meal, Sadie kept scanning the room, not wanting to miss someone famous. Despite an exquisite dining experience, she was a little disappointed that they didn't get to see one of their favorite movie stars. Maybe next time.

A few flutters began in her stomach as the evening came to an end. It wasn't over for her. A late night visit with Vince was the icing on the cake.

"You look all bright-eyed and bushy-tailed. Are you seeing Vince tonight? Maybe another sleepover?" Jill gave a sly little smirk.

Millie opened her eyes wide and moved closer to Sadie.

Sadie didn't want to come across as being rude, so

she confessed, "Yes, I'm stopping by his room later."

"You really like him, don't you?" Millie asked.

"She more than likes him. She slept over, didn't she?" Jill wouldn't give up. "You know I want only the best for you."

"I know you do, honey. It's been a long time coming. We were close in the theater group, but there was nothing more than a friendship. He's always been a great guy and so handsome." She fanned herself.

"We get it." Jill pushed her coffee cup away. "I'm stuffed." She gave a sigh. "I wish Tommy made me feel the way Vince makes you feel. It shows all over your face."

"I'm sorry the spark with Tommy is fading. Maybe you can rekindle it when we get back."

"It needs more than a spark. More like a bonfire." She motioned with her arms spread apart. "I wish we were more compatible."

"You can talk to him about it. If it isn't meant to be, someone else more suited for you will come along," Sadie assured her. She believed her own words, especially since it had happened to her. A wild night with Vince had definitely been unexpected.

A surge of heat swept over her and she took a slow, deep breath. Sadie was glad she'd arranged for the driver to come back for them. He was right on time and parked outside waiting for them.

"That's what I call service," Jill said as they headed to the car.

Once they got buckled in, the driver took off.

Millie yawned. "What's on the agenda for tomorrow?"

"I thought we might go to Universal Studios in the

morning, and the hotel has a van to take us on a tour of the stars' homes. I've always wanted to do it. I packed my expensive camera to take some great pictures." Sadie hoped they didn't think she was being bossy.

"I'm happy you plan things to do. If you left it up to us, we'd be out of luck. We can never make up our minds," Millie admitted.

"Speak for yourself." Jill laughed.

"It's true and you know it," Sadie said with a smile as she patted Jill's hand.

"I suppose I do have a little trouble making decisions." Jill put her head on Sadie's shoulder. "You're so good at it. Thanks for being organized. I'd love to go to the studio and on the tour. Let's leave early. If you don't stay out too late, we can get out early enough to enjoy the whole day."

****

When they got back to the room, Sadie made a beeline for the bathroom. She brushed her teeth and fluffed up her hair. A dap of lip-gloss and she was good to go. Before heading out, she checked her phone messages and deleted the ones she'd already heard. What a thrill to find that Vince had left a voicemail. Her heart soared as she listened to it. He was looking forward to seeing her again. Sadie gripped the phone tight and giggled. She realized she was acting like a teenager, but she'd set out to have fun, and she'd promised herself to live like there was no tomorrow.

Millie and Jill had already changed into their summery pajamas and slippers. The television blared and the two of them were sprawled out on their stomachs across the king-sized bed.

"What are you watching?"

"It's chick flick night." Jill kept her eyes glued on the screen.

"Well, I'm leaving. Wish me luck."

"You don't need luck. Vince is hooked." Jill displayed an okay sign with her fingers.

"Yeah, sure. Thanks for the vote of confidence. We'll see." In her heart, she had a feeling it was true. It was scary to get involved with a guy you thought was only a friend. She'd heard of it happening to other people, but she never dreamed it would happen to her. Everyone said that being friends first was a good thing.

"Have a nice night." Millie plumped her pillows and waved from under the covers.

Jill got up and scooted her along.

"Thanks." Sadie took off like she was in a race.

On the way to his room she moistened her lips, excited to see him. Her belly filled with flutters.

When she knocked on Vince's door he opened it in a flash and greeted her with a welcoming grin. "Come in. You're here earlier than I'd expected." He ushered her inside, closed the door, and held her around the waist.

A five o'clock shadow made him look even hotter than he already did, and in his faded, tight jeans, he couldn't be any cuter.

"I'm sorry I didn't shave again. I was so engrossed in reading. You might as well get used to the real me." He held his arms out.

"I don't see a problem." She stood with one hand on her chin. "You do look great in distressed jeans." If only she could keep her eyes in her head, she wouldn't seem like a stalker. She swooned over the way the jeans hugged his muscular thighs. The form-fitting shirt didn't look too shabby either. They'd spent the night together, had known each other since they were teenagers, and yet her insides still rattled. If he noticed the nervous twitch in her eye, she'd flip. She held her clutch close to her chest.

"Would you like something to drink?" He moved over to the tiny kitchenette and opened the refrigerator door. "There's beer, water, and soda. I almost forgot, a woman sent me a vintage bottle of wine." He motioned to a gift bag on the counter. "It came with a nice note about how much she enjoyed the show."

"How nice of her. You're a bigger star than you think."

"I wouldn't go that far, but I wish."

"I'm in the mood for a glass of wine. Will you join me?" Sadie asked.

"Sure, I'll have one."

"It's been so many years since our days in the theater group. We should have kept in touch."

"If you're not counting the reunion and the time we ran into one another at the grocery store," he added.

Vince checked in a drawer and took out a corkscrew. Once the bottle was open, he grabbed two long-stemmed glasses from the top of the counter and poured the wine. He went over to dim the lights and then he turned on the stereo.

"Much better." He handed Sadie a glass of wine and sat on the sofa, motioning for her to sit next to him.

She sat and took a sip. "This is good." Her tongue darted in and out of her mouth.

"Don't do that unless you want me to kiss you."

"Do what?"

"Stick your tongue out." He gave an admiring grin,

and she shuddered when she got a peek at his dimples.

"I didn't realize I did it. Or are you just trying to find an excuse to make out?" She poked his side and let out a laugh.

"Maybe." He tilted his head, smiling. Draping his arm around her shoulder, he nestled close, giving her arm a gentle squeeze. "Isn't this the life? It's beautiful out tonight, and I'm here with you."

"With the drapes wide open, the evening view is breathtaking. A gorgeous midnight blue sky with pinkish red streaks is as pretty as a painting." Sadie sighed and closed her eyes for a moment, content with Vince by her side. "I never expected to be here with you, but I'm happy we ran into one another."

Being next to Vince was where she wanted to be. His strong hands caressing her arm helped calm her rapid pulse. He nuzzled her neck gently as his lips roamed along her shoulder. A shiver ran down her spine. She'd kept her feelings to herself long enough. This was the right time. Their chance meeting was meant to be. Sadie decided to come clean.

She folded her hands and sat straight up. "I have a confession to make." She was serious. Dead serious. Their relationship would never work based on a lie.

"You do? What is it?" He raised his brows and his smile slopped into a slight frown. He shifted his position. "Go ahead."

"Yes. Umm...I wanted to tell you this last night, but I didn't want to break the mood." She took a deep breath and placed her hand on top of his. "I was attracted to you when we worked together in the theater company. I'm sorry I made you feel like you weren't my type. It was a horrible thing to do."

"No, it wasn't. You never made me feel unaccepted. I thought I was too pushy." He gave her hand a gentle squeeze. "I'm so happy you told me." Vince ran his hand across the top of his head. "God, I thought you were about to tell me you had a boyfriend." He exhaled and seemed to come back to life. "I had a feeling you liked me too. My buddy told me different. That jerk. All these years gone by."

"We're here now, and that's what counts." She put her arms around his neck and tears of joy filled her eyes. It was magnificent to have a second chance at life and at love. The minute she saw his face on the romance novel cover, an array of emotions too difficult to explain filled her body and soul.

He slowly reached for the sides of her face and gazed lovingly into her eyes. Her blood soared through her veins. When he gently lifted her chin and kissed her softly on the lips, she never wanted to let him go. She held her hand on his chest and felt the pounding of his heart. If she'd realized how wonderful falling in love with Vince was, she would have thrown herself at his feet years ago.

Vince sat back and kept his arm around her shoulders. He rested his head back and glanced out at the evening view, gently raking his fingers up and down her arm. Her mind and body relaxed to the magic of his touch.

"Have you heard anything about the show yet?" Sadie asked.

He stirred and turned to face her. "Nope. My manager doesn't want me to get my hopes up. There's so many pilots that never get picked up." Vince shrugged. "For now, I'm not counting on it. Life goes on in the meantime." He slouched down into the upholstery and crossed one leg over the other.

She closed her eyes and an idea popped into her head. It would be nice to have an assistant with the senior play. They worked well as a team. Although, she wouldn't want to impose on him. *He's got to earn a living too, and this job is not a paying one.* She'd wait. Now wasn't the time to make a hasty decision.

"You're awfully quiet all of a sudden." Vince was so in tune with her.

"Oh, I was just thinking of something back home. I'm sorry. I'm all yours. Business set aside until after next Monday."

"Good. I wish I was staying until then. I'm flying back tomorrow." He held his lips tight together.

"You're kidding?" Sadie's whole mood did a complete turnaround. She put on a half-smile and tried to rally. "What time do you check out?"

"My flight is at ten in the morning."

"I'm sorry you have to go home. At least Jersey weather is better now that spring is here."

She tried to stay positive and not come across as overbearing. They'd see each other soon. For heaven's sake, they lived in the same town. Yet their paths were so different. Vince had pursued an acting career, and he traveled regularly into the city for auditions. Sadie had school all day, with her students being a huge part of her life.

"Yeah, that's true. But I'd rather be here with you."

"Oh, you would?"

She felt a little sorry for him. He was extremely talented, and it made her sad to see him struggle to follow his dream. She didn't have the guts to stick to hers. She'd never admit it to anyone, but tucked deep inside, Sadie knew teaching was second best.

"I'm enjoying the music. It's serene and romantic." She nestled up against his chest, his heartbeat next to her ear. The time spent together looking out at the star-filled sky was a moment to cherish. Vince slowly stroked her hair. While she listened to the soft music in the background, Sadie's eyes got heavy.

She stirred to the sound of a cellphone voicemail alert, and she peeked at her watch. It was after two AM. She stretched and found Vince staring at her.

"Hi, sleepyhead," he whispered close to her ear. "We must have fallen asleep. It's funny, we both conked out at the same time." He covered his mouth and yawned.

"I guess we needed the rest. Would you mind if I didn't sleep over? I woke up with a slight headache, and besides, you have to be up and out early."

"I don't mind. You probably want to curl up and sleep until noon. You've been a busy girl, and you've had a rough year. I'm ready to fall back asleep anyway. Neither one of us got much rest last night." Vince offered her an accepting grin.

Sadie stood and picked up her purse from the sleek, gold coffee table. Vince got up and put his arms around her waist. He pulled her close and kissed her as if he were leaving for duty overseas, his soft moans tempting her to stay.

He held onto her and stared into her eyes. "I want to take you out to a nice place for dinner as soon as you get back. On the water maybe. I remember how much you love Spring Lake. After dinner, we can take a stroll on the boardwalk to watch the sunset."

"I'd like that. Do you remember when the bunch of us tried to light a campfire and the police came?"

"I sure do. I had to talk us out of being dragged into headquarters. I think the officer went to school with my father," he recalled.

"It seems so long ago." She smiled and turned to start toward the door.

Vince spun her around for one more kiss. He held her close up against his chest and ran his hand up and down her back, sending an electrifying surge through her. His mouth lingered on hers.

"Have a safe trip. I'll see you soon." Sadie stared into his eyes.

His passionate kiss made her a little tipsy, but Sadie had learned a thing or two about men. Her mother also advised to always keep an element of mystery, and most importantly, don't be clingy. It wasn't easy. How she managed to stay calm and cool, she'd never know. He opened the door and she left with uncertainties floating around in her head.

At least it was the last night she'd have to sneak into her room like a teen who was afraid of being grounded. Sadie craved a good night's rest and time to gather her thoughts. Next week they'd be back in Jersey, and she wondered if things would pick up where they left off or if it was merely a vacation fling.

Millie and Jill were sound asleep when she got in. Sadie slipped into the bathroom to change. She pushed her bangs off her forehead with a headband and washed her face. She brushed her teeth and swished around some minty mouthwash as she stared at herself in the mirror. It was a relief to have a healthy glow back. She had been as pale as a ghost all winter.

Tucked under the covers with her thoughts centered on Vince, it wasn't long before she drifted to sleep.

Chapter 5

Vince opened the door to his studio apartment, set down his bags, and then went back out to get the mail. He wished he'd remembered to ask the landlord to bring it in for him. The apartment house had three rows of mailboxes on the wall a few feet from the front door. He grunted and pushed the door in and lifted the lock forcefully, since the tiny slot was stuffed to the limit. The scent of fresh cut grass ascended through the screen door, and it reminded him of when he was a kid doing lawn work for spending money on Saturday afternoons.

A huge wraparound porch lined with light blue rocking chairs and white wicker tables made the place warm and homey. It was only a couple blocks from the beach, which was the best part about the rental property. He doubted if he'd ever have the nerve to bring Sadie to his place. It was a decent space, if he did a little clean up, but a man his age should have a home of his own by now.

Most of the renters in the house usually stayed short term. Only one of the tenants had lived there for ten years. Miss Molly had the best one-bedroom apartment in the house. It was just her and an older tabby cat. The landlord looked the other way and didn't uphold the no-animal policy with her. Her pet was a house cat, and good old Rocky was the only family she had. Every morning, the friendly woman greeted Vince with a cheery hello from her corner of the porch. She'd sit there for hours and rock as she waved to the people passing by. Molly kept an eye on the comings and goings on the dwelling.

The moment he started back inside, the elderly woman appeared around the corner with a container in her hand. She reminded him of a chef in a hometown eatery with her apron, overstuffed pockets, and a hairnet on her head. He smiled.

"I made an extra batch of potato pancakes. Welcome home," she shouted, her voice raspy, yet enthusiastic. "I took a chance you'd be back." She grinned.

"How generous of you. I happen to love potato pancakes. My grandmother used to make them for me on Sundays." Vince bent down and inhaled the tempting aroma when she opened the top. His mouth watered. "Just like Grandma's. Thank you." He took the container and offered an appreciative grin.

"I put some applesauce on the side." She winked, lifted one shoulder, and shuffled along.

It was nice to have a close group of neighbors, however, Vince didn't plan on being a permanent renter. Years of trying to make it as an actor hadn't produced enough income to purchase a house. At the moment, he had no choice but to live like a college kid, since he never knew if the next job would come through. If the television show was picked up, it would be a life saver. For now, he'd wait tables at the restaurant and maybe shoot a cover or two. The extra money helped pay the bills, although he did wish he'd get to do a cover for a major publisher.

Luckily, Joey had scored two awesome opportunities for him with auditions for potential guest spots on TV shows. And fortunately, the casting was in NYC. One of the roles was as a cop, the other an emergency room resident. Strangely enough, his father had wanted him to go into medicine, even though he never took time to help him with his homework. He'd rather play a doctor on television anyway. Show business had been in his blood since he performed in the grade school talent show. There was nothing like making an audience happy and hearing the sound of their applause.

He left the plate of food on the table in the eating area. If he didn't unpack right away, he'd put if off forever. As Vince hung up his clothes, he couldn't help but think of Sadie. He'd love to hear her voice. Even though it'd only been a few hours, it seemed like an eternity since he'd held her in his arms. He'd fallen hard for her once again, and this time it was reciprocated. After he dropped his dirty laundry into a basket, he went into the bathroom, splashed some water on his face, and washed his hands.

The spicy aroma of onion in the potato pancakes from the kitchen made his mouth water. Vince couldn't resist, and he went over to the table, sat, and opened the container. Luckily, the food was still warm. He took a taste and couldn't help but devour the entire portion in minutes. He'd hit the gym and work his butt off. A rigorous workout had helped him with more than getting his once scrawny body in shape. It also did wonders for his frame of mind.

Once he rinsed the Tupperware, Vince flopped down on a broken-in, down-stuffed love seat and propped a throw pillow behind his head. It was exactly where he wanted to be for the rest of the afternoon. He'd hit the gym after five. The sleeper love seat was worn in just the way he liked it. He reached for the remote.

The sound of the news in the background didn't keep him from daydreaming about the silky soft feel of Sadie's skin when she wrapped her legs around him in bed. She'd evolved into a sexy, sophisticated, and desirable woman. Back in LA, it had taken all his willpower to resist her charm and wait until the right moment. He still couldn't believe she'd made the first move. The sweet sound of her voice was music to his ears. No other woman could come close to reaching into his heart.

He dozed off for a minute and practically fell off the edge when there was a loud banging on the door. He jumped up and opened it to find his mother standing outside.

"I had a day off, so I thought I'd stop by. I remembered you told me you'd be home today."

"Hey, Mom, come on in," he said, relieved it wasn't some sort of emergency in the building.

She stepped inside with her shoulders slumped, her brow tight, and a weary grin on her face. "I hope I'm not interrupting anything."

Vince straightened his shirt and ran a hand over the back of his hair. He didn't like the troubled tone in her voice. He wasn't expecting to see his mom today, and besides, she usually called before a visit. He reached out and offered a hug as she entered the room. Her youthful appearance made him smile. She'd had a makeover downtown at a new salon. Instead of being stuck in the seventies, she was finally up to date in style. Her once mousy brown hair was enhanced with a softer shade of brown with subtle lighter highlights around her face, and she'd allowed her stylist to add bangs.

"I'm surprised, but I'm glad you stopped by." Was there something more to her unannounced appearance at his doorstep? Vince knew her all too well.

"You have a hint of color on your face. It looks like you had time outdoors." She moved around the loveseat and sat.

"I did hang out by the pool whenever I had a few minutes to spare." He gave her a slanted stare, wondering what was up. She was making small talk. Another sign. "Is everything okay? Are you and Dad working things out?" Judging by the tears in her eyes, Vince had a hunch he was right on target.

"He's making progress, and he even did some of the work around the house. It saved me from having to hire a contractor." She fidgeted in her seat.

"I hope he knows how lucky he is," Vince said.

He'd never gotten into a fight with his father. That wasn't his sort of thing; kindness went a long way. But it annoyed the hell out of him how his father let his drinking ruin his family life. His mother had sacrificed for years.

"Mom, it's time for you to take care of yourself. You've done your best." He clenched his jaw and played with his watch, annoyed, yet hopeful.

What did it take for a grown man with a wonderful wife to get his act together?

It wasn't worth the energy it took to stay mad. Vince took a couple of slow, deep breaths. He wasn't going to make his dad's afflictions the focus.

One thing that scared Vince was the way he was still following his dreams instead of getting a steady nine-to-five job. Just like his father had done. When he was in grade school, his father had repeatedly chased the dream of owning an eighteen wheeler. He'd stay home with a beer can in one hand and draw sketches of the way he wanted the cab of his rig to look instead of pounding the pavement to support his family. Was he more like his father than he'd like to admit? His gut twisted at the thought.

"I'm sorry to seem impatient." He sat and put his arm around her shoulder. All he wanted was to offer support and comfort. His father had fallen off the wagon since he was in grade school. Once his idol, now Vince was embarrassed to be seen with him.

"I understand. I'm going to meetings and my support group are helping me learn to say no. I'm doing much better, really. Daddy is doing much better too." She shifted and then crossed her legs. "Tell me more about your trip. I don't want to spend our visit talking about your father." She put on a smile.

"Well, I hope he keeps it up and does the right thing." He glanced down and then turned toward her. "I'm sorry. It was a huge relief that the show got a good reception from the LA audience, but I'm not getting my hopes up." He shrugged, picked up a pack of sugarless gum from the end table, and popped a piece into his mouth. "You know how many of these things get canned?" A dose of showbiz blues about being back to the drawing board set in, nevertheless, he forced a smile.

"I know how much it means to you and how hard

you work. Have you had any auditions for the theater, your first love? Grandma's help with voice training wasn't wasted, was it? It enhanced your already beautiful musical abilities," she bragged.

Vince found it amusing how his mother still put him on a pedestal. He wished it was as simple as she made it sound. "I go on auditions for the theater all the time. Besides the chorus in the few I've done, nothing else comes through. I haven't even been lucky enough to get a call back for a supporting role. I'm too tall, too short, not thin enough, or wrong for the role in every which way. My agent makes sure to get the feedback."

He faced facts. The men in their twenties usually snagged the roles. Thirty was the age when you had to fight harder to stand out. But he was determined to stay on top of his game.

"Don't worry. I'm not giving up, but I have to keep plugging away at whatever comes along."

"That's the spirit," his mother said, her tone uplifted. "I have faith in you, and I'm so proud of your determination." She reached over and squeezed his hand. "I'm behind you all the way, and I can't wait to hear more about how you ran into Sadie."

Vince knew he wasn't going to be able to get off the hook. He pursed his lips. There wasn't much he could share about his relationship with Sadie so early on…if they even had one once she returned from her trip.

He shrugged. "We had some laughs, and Sadie and a couple of girlfriends came to see me perform."

"That's nice. Is that it? It seems as if there's more to the story. Oh, I'm sorry, it's none of my business," she sputtered.

"We had dinner one night, and that is about it." A guy with a beat-up old Honda who lived paycheck to paycheck wasn't exactly a woman's idea of the perfect catch. The illusion of a model/TV star got him by in LA, but back in the real world, he wasn't there yet. After a reluctant sigh, he stood and went over to the refrigerator. "Do you want something to drink?" He took out a bottle of iced tea. "I'll split it with you."

"Yes, I'd like one."

Vince grabbed two paper cups from the cabinet next to the sink. He dropped a few ice cubes in each one. An ice cold tea was the next best thing to a frosty mug of beer on an unseasonably warm spring day.

"I have a box of your favorite ginger snaps. Do you want one?" he asked. His mother had always packed a picnic lunch for outings to the beach when Vince was in elementary school, and always included the spicy cookies. He'd taken a liking to them.

"Why not? I didn't have much of a lunch," she replied.

He carried her tea and the cookies over to a straw chest he used for a coffee table and placed them down before going back to get his tea.

"Sit next to me," she insisted as she took a bite of the ginger cookie.

Vince sat and reached over for a cookie. He popped half of it into his mouth.

"You seem different, happier," his mother said as she took a sip of her drink.

"I am, despite the daily grind." He sat up straight and flashed a smile. Vince was lucky to have such a strong and positive woman in his life to help him see the bright side of things. He'd realized running into

Sadie also had something to do with his drive. She was the one missing link in his life, and now that he'd found her again, nothing was going to hold him back.

"You've always pushed hard and fought for what you wanted. I have total faith you'll get all that you want and more. You're talented and all of your hard work will pay off. I'm sure of it." Her words sounded like part of a dissertation.

"Thanks, Mom. How can you be so sure?" He'd like to believe her encouraging words, but he knew she didn't have a crystal ball she could gaze into. She was his biggest cheerleader, and he appreciated her constant support. He yawned. His hectic schedule had caught up to him.

"You're welcome. You are an extremely talented actor and your determination will pay off."

He smiled at her. "You supported me emotionally when I needed it badly. Do you remember a few years back when I considered giving up acting and opting for a nine-to-five job instead? You encouraged me not to throw in the towel."

"Of course I remember. I stand by it." She sipped her tea.

The vision of being dressed in a three-piece suit with a tie and a briefcase in his hand still haunted him. It'd be near torture to force him to conform. He had to accept the fact that an actor's life has its fair share of ups and downs. You could count on a roller coaster ride, doors slammed in your face, long days for little pay, and taking side jobs as a model to keep food on the table. However, he didn't have a choice. It was all he knew and all he ever wanted.

His cellphone blared, and he answered it on the

first ring. Vince was surprised to hear from his manager so early in the day. "Hey, buddy. Any news?"

"It's too soon, but I'm keeping my fingers crossed. Hang in there. I was calling to see if you got in."

"Yup. I'm safe and sound. Let me know as soon as you get word." Vince gave a groan as he ended the call. "I was hoping he'd heard something, but no such luck."

"Don't give up," she insisted in a supportive tone. "You hear me?"

He stood, rubbed the back of his neck, and scanned the tiny living space he'd called home for three years. Renewed determination gave him enough energy to see the bright side of his journey. His life was turning around. He wouldn't let fear or insecurity over his shortcomings get in the way. Flashy cars and an elaborate lifestyle weren't the way to prove your worth. He was certain Sadie was not about status or money. He hoped she knew his heart was sincere. He would prove they were right for one another.

"I'll go so you can get some rest. You must be exhausted."

"I am tired. I'll see you out." Vince accompanied his mother to the door.

"I'd love to have you and Sadie over for dinner." She gave a cheeky grin.

How was she so sure he'd see her again? He'd only told her that they *might* pick things up once they got home, but his mother seemed to be certain it would happen. He shook his head, trying not to laugh. "I'll call you."

"See you soon." She gave him a goodbye hug and was on her way.

****

Daydreaming about Vince made her energized. Sadie was up early, dressed, and eager to begin the day. Seated in front of the window, she positioned her hand on her throat and closed her eyes, reliving each glorious moment of the night they'd spent together. It went to show how things could change in a heartbeat. So far the trip had exceeded her expectations. She had so much to look forward to.

The girls were fortunate to have another beautiful day to explore LA. After checking the schedule they decided to do the tour of the stars' homes first then maybe go on to Universal Studios or Rodeo Drive. She couldn't wait to take a ride on a train through a movie set.

Dressed in a pair of white cropped pants, a navy blue lightweight jacket, and a striped V-neck tank, Sadie was excited to set out on another adventure. While she waited for Millie and Jill to get dressed, she reached into her tote bag and took out the book flap she'd picked up in the promo aisle. She stared at the photo of Vince as she held it up to the light and ran her finger across it. A warmth traveled through her body as she studied every inch of his sculpted chest. She'd be back his strong arms soon. Good thing she had the memento to hold onto until they met again back home. It took time to process everything, nevertheless, she couldn't wait to see where it all led.

"I'm ready." Jill spun around and modeled her designer clothes. "How do you like it?"

"It's definitely you, and you look fabulous," Sadie said.

"I hope so. It was ridiculously expensive." She sashayed over to the bed and picked up her purse. "Are you ready, Millie?"

Millie sat at the vanity and put the finishing touches on her makeup. "I'm glad the hotel has this extra feature. I can never get into the bathroom." She shook her head and dropped a lipstick and a compact into her bag. "I'm finished." She stood.

Sadie strolled over to the window and stared out at the Hollywood sign.

"Are you with us?" Jill asked as she tapped her foot. "You look all googly-eyed. You must be thinking about your man. You'll see him soon enough. Today is girls' day on the tour bus."

Sadie laughed. "Very funny. I'm sorry. Yes, let's go. This is going to be so much fun. I've always wanted to ride through Beverly Hills and get a glimpse of the multimillion dollar homes." She recalled the days when her one of her wildest dreams was to be cast as the female lead in the movies. It seemed so very long ago.

With her crossover bag in place, she got up and followed her friends out.

****

Jill slid down in the seat next to Sadie, and Millie sat across from them. The driver shut his door, buckled up, and they were on their way in a cute little pink tour bus.

"I'm surprised there's only one other person on the tour," Jill whispered.

A young woman with a backpack on the seat next to her was alone in the front seat.

"I wonder why she's by herself. She looks like a kid." Sadie stretched her neck to get a better look.

"Why do you seem so sad? You're not smiling, and you got awfully quiet all of a sudden." Jill gave Sadie a nudge. "I thought you wanted to do this."

"I did. I mean I do."

"It's that dude from your theater group, isn't it? You fell for him."

"It's not that." Sadie sighed.

"Then what is it?"

"Being with Vince reminds me of how much I wanted to be an actress and how I settled." Her voice trembled as she picked a piece of lint off her capris.

"What do you mean? You're a great teacher, and you enjoy your career," Millie joined in. "I see how you light up when your kids are onstage. Sometimes our plans change for a reason."

"I know. Thanks, you two. Vince is a great guy. I can't wait to see where it goes from here." There was no denying her feelings, yet all the talk about her theater days still made her squirm. She played with her earring.

"Is he good in bed?" Jill blurted out.

"All I'll say is I can relax with him, and he is the most caring and gentle man," she proudly announced.

"It's an important part of a relationship," Millie said. "I'm happy for you."

"It sure is. Here we are." Jill put her face close to the window. "Would you look at these places? I'd give anything to have one of these homes."

Once the driver turned into the estate section, Sadie tried to clear her head. She'd finally made it to the exclusive area. "The houses are unbelievable. One is prettier than the next." She stared out the window and took her camera out and began clicking away. "I'm getting some great pictures. I hope I can remember who lives where."

"Write it down. House number one, and so forth." Jill raised her brows. "You're usually the one who pays attention to details." She chuckled.

The driver pulled over to the side of the road, turned off the van, and stood. He was dressed professionally, wearing dark pants and a jacket. His friendly smile put Sadie at ease, and his voice was as deep as a television announcer.

"Who thinks they know the name of the star from the fifties who once lived in this home?" He motioned to direct their attention to a uniquely designed mansion.

Sadie rubbed the side of her forehead and searched for an answer. Since she'd read everything she could get her hands on about old Hollywood, she should be able to guess. His inquiry stumped her, even though she was up on her celebrity news. Millie and Jill sat still and as quiet as if they were in church.

When no one raised their hand, he explained how Fred Astaire had the bachelor pad built after his first wife died. He began a story about the neighborhood and the exclusive parties, and in between, he slipped in tidbits of a couple of scandalous tales. His interesting facts intrigued Sadie, and it helped her focus, instead of letting her surfacing doubts about Vince's career coming between them ruin the day. Before long, she was laughing along with her friends.

The lone traveler had moved closer to them, and she explained that she was on a sabbatical, traveling from Ireland. Sadie found her decision to set out on an adventure inspiring. She wished she'd done something as brave when she was her age. For whatever reason, her fight spirit was dwindling. What happened to living in the moment? She'd started out good when she made the first move with Vince. Why was she all of a sudden second-guessing everything? She was guilty of overthinking as usual. Old habits were hard to break. Not today. This was Hollywood.

While they continued the tour, the three friends wiggled around in their seats as if they were kids on a school trip. The allure of Beverly Hills made a lasting impression on Sadie. "This area is so different from our sleepy little town of Point Pleasant." She let out a soft sigh.

"I'm glad you suggested the tour," Millie admitted.

"It was fun. Let's contact the limo driver when we get back. We can go in style to Rodeo Drive." Sadie searched her purse for his card. "Here it is. I'm going to call him."

"Why not? We deserve the best." Millie gave a firm nod.

"If you insist." Jill giggled as she applied her lip-gloss and put on her designer sun glasses.

The driver let them out and tipped his hat. "Thank you, ladies. Watch your step."

Once they were back inside the hotel, Sadie sat next to the fountain and dialed the limo driver who had given her his card. "I hope he's available."

"We'll be at the coffee shop." Millie and Jill slipped away.

They were in luck. The driver had free time and he was picking them up in fifteen minutes. Sadie hurried over to the coffee shop to announce the good news.

"Our chariot will arrive in a few minutes," she gloated.

"Here, we ordered your favorite." Jill handed her a latte.

"You're a doll. Thank you. Let's take our drinks outside. We don't want to make our driver wait."

The three of them strutted across the lobby and sat outside on the elegantly designed seating area along the perimeter of the hotel. They sipped their coffee and waited.

"Here he is," Sadie announced and stood. She tossed her cup in a nearby trash container as Millie and Jill did the same.

The driver got out and opened the back door. "Where to?"

"Rodeo Drive, please." She smiled as they climbed in the back of the limo.

He closed the door, hopped in the driver's seat, and slowly pulled out onto the street.

"Let's have lunch and then shop 'til we drop," Millie suggested.

"I'm starved. Maybe we can sit outside. It's such a gorgeous day." Sadie's stomach growled.

Bright streaks of light ascended down on the windshield, and she reached into her purse for her sunglasses. She slipped them on and settled back. People dressed in lightweight clothes lined the streets, and the pep in their steps was so opposite from the frantic pace of the folks back home. She could definitely get used to this lifestyle.

When a text came through, she slid her finger across the screen. Her heart skipped a beat when she saw it was from Vince. Sadie careful read it as she chewed on her lip, making sure not to miss a single word. The day couldn't get any better. He apologized for interrupting her plans and wrote how much he missed her already. He added two hearts and a kiss. She immediately replied with a smiley face and a heart.

Even though her relationship with Vince brought her back to a time she'd like to shove deep inside, she wasn't going to let it destroy something as beautiful as what they'd found. He was all that she'd ever wanted in a man, and she wasn't going to give him up. She'd never experienced such deep feelings for anyone she'd dated before. When he held her in his arms, nothing else mattered. The whole experience had unfolded the way she'd always believed love should be. It was something out of a fairy tale, and after the stressful year she'd survived, it was exactly what she needed.

Rodeo Drive was a shopping paradise. The Torso statue was the first thing she spotted. It sat in the divider on the street, and Sadie hurried to snap a picture. The top-of-the-line boutiques were lined up, and she couldn't wait to have lunch and shop. Her budget was tight, but she'd managed to put a few extra dollars away to splurge. Her mother had forced her to take a handout, even though she'd resisted. She'd bring her back something special. They crossed the street to an area filled with all types of cool looking places to eat.

"This is more exciting than I'd imagined," Sadie said. It was better than being on a Christmas shopping spree on Cyber Monday. "I have to go into the Hermes store." She put the shop first on her list. Since college, Sadie loved the unique and exotic fragrances. It was unlike the scents most commonly worn by women her age, and she liked being different.

In the days before she had decided to give up an acting career, she used to buy her fragrances in New York City. A fleeting memory of an audition for an off-

Broadway show popped into her head, but she shook it off. It seemed so long ago. Rejection was not easy. These days she didn't have to deal with it, and that suited her just fine.

"Wow! Do you see the car that just parked? I think it's someone famous." Sadie gulped. She bobbed in and out of the crowd gathering on the sidewalk.

"Wait for us." Jill put her arm through Millie's.

"It's a once-in-a-lifetime opportunity to get a glimpse of a real-life movie star up close and personal. I see her. It's the writer from *Sex and the City*. You know…Carrie."

"You're right," Millie replied.

"She's prettier than she is on television." Sadie tried not to stare.

A potted plant was in the way of a good view of the actress as she exited the car, and maybe it was a good thing. She scurried into a restaurant. This way they couldn't gawk.

"How cool was that?" Sadie stood in front of the eatery. "We couldn't get in there if we tried. Too exclusive. You'd probably have to wait a year to get a reservation." Her shoulders dropped.

"Shopping will take your mind off of it. Come, girls, the shoes are calling." Jill pranced ahead. "Let's get a little shopping therapy in before we have lunch."

"I have an idea. There's a deli on the corner. How about we grab a wrap or something quick? That will give us more time to hit the stores," Sadie pointed out.

"That sounds like plan B. I'm in," Jill said.

"Me too," Millie agreed.

The girls trotted across the street and got in line. Turkey wraps with arugula and balsamic dressing for three had the perfect amount of protein to energize them for the afternoon. Huddled at a counter by the window, they gulped down their food and then carried their soft drinks outside.

"After we see as much as we can here, let's ask the driver to take us down the Sunset Strip. We can get a glimpse of the famous rock clubs, and then we can stop at one of those yummy cupcake places," Sadie eagerly suggested.

"Did I hear cupcakes?" Jill gave a wide-eyed grin.

"Yes, by then we'll need a pick-me-up." Sadie smiled back.

"I can't wait to window-shop, and maybe I'll splurge." Millie applied her lip-gloss.

"Let's do a selfie. Get ready." Sadie moved close to her friends and took the photo.

Then it was off to shopping heaven.

****

"What a fun day. Sorry, ladies, I'm first." Jill rushed into the bathroom.

Sadie dropped her bags on the bed. She searched through them.

Millie sat at the table and looked over a few souvenirs she'd purchased. "I hope my mother likes these." She lifted up a perfume and a package of fancy soaps.

"She'll love it," Sadie said.

Jill came out, sat on the edge of the bed, and kicked her shoes off.

"I'm going to freshen up." Sadie carried the bag from Hermes and ran into the bathroom. She grabbed the plush bath towel from the rack and wiped the steam off the mirror. The bar of soap from her favorite shop smelled wonderful. It made a rich and silky lather, and it felt great on her face.

She touched her cheeks and noticed how her skin glowed. Was it the sun or the fact that she was so happy? Maybe a little of both. Since it was nearly summer, and it was her favorite time of year, Sadie pictured herself strolling hand and hand along the shore with Vince. She sighed, hoping she wasn't thinking too far ahead.

A shrill scream from the other room startled her. Her hands shook. As she hurried to open the bathroom door, her heart pounded. Jill and Millie ran around the room in circles.

"What's going on?" Sadie shouted.

"Johnny Marks and his band are downstairs. We heard a group of teenagers talking about it in the hallway when we went out to grab a couple of snacks from the vending machines."

Jill spoke so fast Sadie had to turn her ear toward her to understand what she was babbling about. She waved her hands in the air like a crossing guard.

"Hurry! We'll meet you downstairs." Millie was out of breath.

"Take it easy." Sadie laughed. "That's okay. I'll skip this one." At the moment, Sadie had only one man on her mind, and no one could compare. Not even a rock star.

"You love Johnny Marks. Are you sure?" They both stared at her like she had two heads.

"Yes, go ahead. Have fun. Get me an autograph." Jill and Millie dashed out of the room.

Sadie changed into a pair of shorts, and slipped on a silky scoop neck tank top, before she realized her phone was ringing.

"I'm sorry. I couldn't wait to hear your voice. Do you mind?" Vince said.

Her head buzzed and her stomach rumbled. She flopped on the bed as excited as a teenager on a first date. "Don't think twice about it. I was going to call you." She giggled. "Did you have a good flight?"

"It wasn't bad. It takes a while to get used to the time change. How was your day?"

"Great. We went on a tour of the stars' homes, and then had lunch on Rodeo Drive. I got my shopping fix for the year."

"Sounds like you had fun. I wish I was still there with you. Did I interrupt anything?"

It was so good to hear from him. "Not a thing. I just hopped out of the shower."

"Now I really wish I was there." He gave a throaty laugh.

"I wish you were here too." Her heart skipped a beat as she played with her hair.

"I haven't heard anything about the show yet, but I'm trying to think positive. Nothing is written in stone, but I might have another great opportunity. I'm waiting to hear back."

"When will you know what the decision on the pilot is?" She tried to keep her tone sincere. If he had to work in LA, any chance of a commitment was doomed. A long-distance relationship was not what she'd had in mind, besides the statistics were not in their favor. Her cousin had waited for her fiancé to finish his degree in a school miles away. She found him in his bed with his classmate on a surprise visit. So much for surprises.

"This may be a little premature. It may still fall

through. My agent got me an audition for a Broadway show. How funny is that?"

"You're on a roll, Vince. Why is it funny?" She dangled her legs over the side of the bed.

"I've been auditioning forever, with one rejection after the other. I'm still going to give it a shot. I've got nothing to lose. The restaurant can survive without me, and a cover shoot only takes a day."

"Wow! So much has happened in such a short time. Good for you." She wanted desperately to make this work. "I know something will come through. You're too talented for it not to," she said with conviction.

"How sweet of you. Thank you. If you were here, I'd kiss you."

"I'd kiss you back," she responded. Goosebumps formed on her arms.

"I'm holding next Sunday open for you. It's the perfect time for our Spring Lake date. How about it? It brings back memories of the days we hung out down the shore."

"I'd love it." His invite reached in and touched her heart in a way she couldn't explain. He'd remembered how she loved the old seashore town with its beautiful homes, quaint shops, and a stroll along a serene beach with the sound of the waves crashing.

"Does the Breeze Inn at seven sound good?" Vince asked with an optimistic tone.

"It sounds fantastic."

A flurry of butterflies hit her stomach. The thought of spending time with Vince in the romantic seashore town made her knees weak. A man who paid attention to special little things like a favorite restaurant, and most of all went all out to please a woman, was not a man to give up on when things didn't go exactly as planned. She'd never do anything to hold him back from pursuing an acting career. He needed encouragement and support, and she was going to give it to him. Sadie secretly hoped he'd agree to help her with the school play if it fit into his schedule.

"I'm going to run. It's time to get outside and clear my head. A jog on the beach is what I need," he said.

"Enjoy it. I'll talk to you soon."

She'd love to be back in New Jersey with him, however, she still had things to see in LA. When she hung up, she put on some blush and lip-gloss, a touch of mascara, and hurried out to meet the girls. She'd join them downstairs to sneak a peek at Johnny Marks, if it wasn't too late.

Chapter 6

Vince left the window open next to his bed, and he pushed the sheer navy panels apart to let in the cool ocean air. It'd been a long day, and it felt good to crawl into his own bed.

He lifted the red, white, and blue patch quilt his grandmother had made for him when he'd graduated high school up to his chest. He could still smell the lilac scent from her garden. He missed his grandma and wished she was there to cheer him on. Her love of quilting kept her busy even into her eighties. She had always used patriotic designs, since his grandpa was a war hero.

The sound of the crickets outside helped him unwind. If only Sadie was alongside of him. Being with Sadie seemed as natural as taking a breath. He'd show her how much she meant to him this time around. Nothing was going to stand in his way. Second chances didn't come along every day, and he wasn't going to mess it up this time.

He grabbed onto an extra pillow and held it close with thoughts of Sadie lying next to him, until he drifted off to sleep.

The sound of a rock anthem blaring from the place upstairs woke Vince, and he strained to make out the time on the nightstand. One thing about the boarding house he didn't like was the thin walls. An apartment change might come sooner than he thought.

He mumbled a few choice words, threw off the covers, and stretched. He had to hurry, since it was after eight. If he wanted to get back to his normal routine of jogging on the beach bright and early, he'd better set an alarm next time. His inner clock was still on LA time. Vince jumped out of bed and went into the bathroom. He washed his face and brushed his teeth, then he threw on a pair of shorts and a muscle tee. He grabbed a protein shake from the refrigerator, guzzled it, slicked his hair back before he put on a baseball hat, and was out the door. He'd try to fit in a workout at the gym another day. He didn't want to lose momentum

With a slow, easy jog, he kicked up the gravel in the driveway as he headed toward the beach. The familiar sight of the shaded, tree-lined streets with pastel-painted homes, some with wraparound porches, and wildflower gardens never got old. The salty scent of the ocean was refreshing. Living down The Jersey Shore had a strong effect on his mood. It brought him peace and comfort. People were friendly and supportive, and life was a little slower here. He enjoyed the frenzy of The Big Apple, but going home to a peaceful place was the right move for him. He'd travel for long lengths of time if his work required his relocating temporarily, yet he'd always return to the seashore town he grew up in. The sound of waves hitting the shore greeted him as he made it up to the boardwalk.

After the jog, Vince had planned to practice his vocal prior to the audition in NYC. He'd have enough time to perfect the chords before he had to catch the train. So many amazing opportunities had come along all at once. He wanted to reach out and make one of them his own. This time he'd get to the next level.

Vince made a mental note to touch base with his mother when he got back from the beach. She was a strong woman and could take care of herself, nevertheless, he wanted to be sure she was okay. Her surprise visit yesterday got him thinking. Tucked in a corner of his heart, he wished his father success with his recovery. It was never too late. Somehow, having Sadie back in his life opened his eyes to what really matters. Family was important, no matter what. Resentments were only in the way of progress and individual growth. His counselor would be so proud of his revelation. Not that he didn't always have it inside of him. He'd needed a push in the right direction, that was all. It all seemed so clear now. He'd heard love does crazy things, and if this change was love, anything was possible.

Once he reached the water's edge, Vince picked up speed. The sea air invigorated him. There were only a few people with the same idea. He was glad it wasn't crowded during the week until summer. The gulls flew in circles overhead, swooping down to search for nibbles of whatever they could find. He enjoyed the ocean breeze on his skin and, with the sky as clear as a painting without a cloud in sight, he'd jog a little farther. He sure hoped the good weather held up for his date with Sadie.

Back at his place, Vince took a quick shower. Wrapped in a lightweight robe, he sang a few bars from the songs in his repertoire before he got ready. His voice was in good form. *I've got this.* It took an hour to feel confident doing the song he chose to perform. He picked up his phone from the kitchen table and dialed his mom. He went over to the sofa and sat.

"Hey, how are you doing?" Vince asked.

"I'm fine. How's your day going? Any news?"

"I'm going to the city today. I don't know if you remember about my audition."

"Of course I remember. I was going to call to wish you luck. You know, I have a good feeling about it."

"You always have a good feeling about my auditions." He appreciated her confidence in him.

"I mean it. I had a dream about Grandma. She was sitting in a theater applauding as you took a bow."

"You probably had our conversation on your mind before you went to bed. Thanks for the positive thoughts. Are you okay? I mean, has Dad been behaving?" He played with the salt and pepper shaker.

"Yes, he has. I'm in a good place, and you don't have to worry another second. You do your best. Let me know how it goes."

"Okay. I was thinking I'd try to have a long talk with Dad one of these days."

"That's what I was hoping. He is your father. He's still going to meetings, and he's even working with a sponsor."

"Great. I better run. Talk to you later."

He'd decided on dark blue jeans and a short-sleeve royal blue shirt. He grabbed his keys, cellphone, and his briefcase with his photos, sheet music, and his publicity packet. He scanned the room to make sure he hadn't forgotten anything. He hoped the train was on time. So far, things seemed to be in his favor. Vince vowed to stay optimistic. He'd made ends meet with modeling, and with two potential acting roles insight and a woman like Sadie in his corner, he had no reason to doubt good things were headed his way. As he was about to walk out of the door to go the train station, he got a call from Joey.

"Hey, buddy."

"Got a minute?" Joey asked.

"Sure. What's up?"

"Sorry to call last minute. I wanted to wish you luck. My man with the show has faith that you're what they want."

"What do you mean?" Vince swallowed hard. He went over to the counter, pulled out a stool, and sat. His head buzzed.

"They caught a glimpse of you in the off-Broadway production the night you got to step in for the lead, and they think you might be what they're looking for. You go and prove you've got what it takes," Joey said with confidence.

"That's a big deal." He felt like he was in a dream. What a break. "I sure will, man. Thanks for having faith in me. I won't let you down."

"I know you won't. Before you go, I spoke to an executive about the pilot. It seems like a decision might take a while. So, what I'm trying to say is this Broadway show might be a blessing in disguise. It will put you out there and give you the break you deserve. And as far as the pilot goes, the timing would allow you to do both. Anyway, you can't count on the show. You know how picky and fickle the networks can be." He cleared his throat.

"Are you feeling okay?"

"Yeah. Just a bit of dust. That's all. Don't worry about me. I can take care of myself, but thanks for caring."

"You know I'm here if you need me."

"Get your butt moving. You've got to be in tip-top shape for today."

"Aye-aye." If they'd been face to face, he felt like a salute would be needed.

His agent gave him guidance above and beyond his realm of duties. He'd helped shape his career with his heart and soul. This was a great opportunity, and he was thankful for Joey's constant support. All of the years he'd been in the business, he'd hoped that the right person would be in the audience and pluck him out of the show. Waiting with patience for what he wanted was starting to pay off in more ways than one. His heart filled with hope and he had just enough anxiety to help keep him on his toes.

Vince jumped in his car, buckled up, and rode along with the heat beating through his sunroof. He popped in the CD of the song he'd prepared and sang along. He couldn't wait to share every detail with Sadie. He'd wait until he knew for sure and it was the right moment to make it about him. Today, it was more important for her to enjoy her time with her friends.

Once he squeezed into a parking spot, he hurried to the platform. He checked the board with the schedule. The train pulled in right on time. In minutes, he had boarded and was on his way.

Vince had more confidence this time. On the last audition for a play, he'd been jittery and unprepared. This romance thing did wonders for his self-esteem. It was strange how everything changed when you found the right partner. Sadie knew him so well—really knew him—and she believed in him. It was exactly what he'd needed to give him the extra boost. He'd do the same for her. She was a giving and loving woman, and he was sure her students adored her. There must be a way he'd be able to lend a hand with her senior production. But he wouldn't say anything to her until he knew for sure he would have the time to do it. The last thing he wanted to do was let Sadie down.

Vince sat next to the window and stared out of it. He envisioned the way Sadie crinkled up her nose when she laughed. Her beauty and sweet disposition had won his heart. She was the kind of woman to build a life with, and the type you'd be able to take home to meet your mother. Luckily, his mother already loved her. Hopefully, he'd reconcile with his father one day soon, once he'd gained enough clean time, and then and only then would Vince bring him around Sadie.

Back in the old days when they'd perform, his father never showed up at a performance. Not even once. Vince had buried the sadness and feelings of rejection deep inside his heart. He greatly appreciated how his mother and grandmother gave him support, and he'd never questioned his dad about why he never showed up. Broken promises had been a daily occurrence at his house. This new-fangled notion to forgive his dad was a surprise even to him. Sure, he'd questioned his own motives. A time in grade school popped into his mind when his father had picked him up because he was sick with a sore throat, took him home, and tucked him into bed. Later, he surprised him with a junior guitar and a few of his favorite ice pops. For now, Vince was at peace with his decision.

****

When the casting director called his name, Vince

squared his shoulders and strode to center stage. He handed his portfolio to an assistant. She was a stylish, older woman with black hair and red highlights, dressed in a pair of skinny jeans. Her warm smile set him at ease. There were also quite a few familiar faces in the room, and besides, people in the business were usually friendly.

"Thank you, honey. Please, take your mark."

He'd been disappointed with the turnout on so many previous attempts on Broadway roles. Maybe this time he'd get his big break. There was something different about this audition. The role was suited for him. People say things happen when they are supposed to happen. There just might be some truth in the old adage. He felt the heat from the lights on his face. Out of the corner of his eye, he spotted one of the producers peering over his glasses and whispering to the person next to him. His heart pounded. It could be a good sign.

He took a sip of water before he began. An inner strength and a deep desire to succeed guided him through. After a few minutes, it was time for him to do his solo vocal. Vince stepped over to a bench where he'd put his briefcase, opened it, and took out his music. He handed it to the young woman behind the piano. She offered an optimistic grin and a wink. *Here goes.* Vince gave it his all, and he felt like he'd really impressed them. He looked out at the vast space, adrenaline surging through his body like a wildfire. The stage was where he belonged. His voice fit the role like it was made for him. His range was high enough to hit the notes. His confidence seemed stronger this time around.

His positive attitude must have showed in his

performance. The producer wanted him to sing again, this time with the female lead. She'd been chosen beforehand and was already well established in the theater world. If he got the part, he'd work hard to prove himself. Although he'd be crazy busy and might not get to spend as much time with Sadie. It would all be worth it in the end. He hoped she'd understand. Not that he had any of the jobs yet. It'd probably be better if he didn't speculate. He couldn't wait to tell Sadie everything about the audition and how amazing the theater was.

He carefully examined the expressions of the people in the front rows, trying to speculate. All eyes were on him. Vince felt a queasiness develop in his gut. There was so much at stake. Last time wasn't this difficult. He exhaled. Now that he knew he'd been considered for the part, it made it real for him. His dream was getting closer to becoming a reality. Damn, he knew this play inside and out. He crossed his fingers and hoped his inkling was on target.

****

The girls slept late and decided to order breakfast in. The array of pastries, croissants, homemade jams, gourmet muffins, coffee, and fresh fruits was fit for royalty. They sat around a table covered in a white linen tablecloth with an arrangement of spring flowers in the center next to the wall of windows in their room.

"This is the life." Jill flipped her hair as she sipped a Mimosa.

"It sure is. I'm having the best time. Thank you for the trip of a lifetime. What a spread. It all smells so good." Sadie picked a cranberry orange muffin and cut it in half. "I feel like I'm in bakery heaven." She smiled as she stared out at the massive city. She took a deep breath, feeling more at peace with her life than she had in a long time.

Millie raised her glass and offered a toast. "To friendship, and to our blessings."

"Thank you." Sadie took a sip of her drink. "It's so good." She ran her tongue along her lips.

"Isn't it great to be all together?" Jill reached over and took a banana nut muffin out of the basket, buttered it, and took a bite. "I could get used to this." She chuckled.

"You and me both." Sadie sampled a strawberry dipped in vanilla yogurt.

"Who would have thought you'd meet a man from your past here in LA?" Millie smiled as she piled a few pieces of fruit on her plate.

"You're in love with him, aren't you?" Jill blurted out of the blue.

"I think it's a little soon to say the word love." In her heart, she knew what she felt.

Vince was different than anyone she'd ever dated. He possessed all of the qualities she'd admired in a man, like honesty, integrity, strength, yet he wasn't afraid to show his emotions. During their time together in the theater, they'd faced challenges, and he gave her support and his undivided attention when she needed it. She didn't want to jump ahead and jinx their relationship. Some of her co-workers had shared tales of confessing their feelings too soon and scaring their men away. She'd try to take it slow. Sadie was afraid she might blink and wake up to find it had just been an amazing dream.

"You had a connection when you were in the

theater, so it's not as if you just met. All of these years Vince never forgot you, and you him. Am I right?"

Millie always said the wisest things. Sadie's eyes filled with a few tears.

"Tell the truth, sweetie. We're here for you," Jill said in a softer tone.

Their concern was well appreciated. "I know you are. All right. Here it is. I've never forgotten Vince either. It's just that our lives took different turns, and we moved on. I never thought he'd still be single. I'd heard most of the members of the group are married. No one really keeps in touch, and time went by so fast." She took another sip of her breakfast pick-me-up. "Vince was shy, and that's what appealed to me the most. He didn't act like other guys who were as good looking as he was, and believe me, he was adorable, but he wasn't a show-off like some of the jocks. I like his sensitive and artsy personality. He drove me wild when we did our love scenes." She giggled. "I never knew he wanted me too. Vince never asked me out or let on that he had a crush on me. I thought he wasn't interested. All that time we shared the same feelings for one another." It was such a relief to get her emotions out. She sighed and gave them a tiny grin.

"That sounds like something out of a movie. You're so lucky, and you deserve every bit of it," Millie said.

Jill crossed her arms and tilted her head, with an expression on her face as if she had just witnessed a bride and groom at the altar. "Beautifully said."

'When are you going to see him again?" Millie spooned herself another portion of fruit.

"He's taking me to my favorite restaurant in Spring

Lake on Sunday." She couldn't contain her excitement. Her speech sped up. "I know exactly what I'm going to wear, and with a tan, the dress will look perfect. I can't wait." She held her arm up and asked, "Do you think I'm tan enough?" She'd wanted to discuss her good news since last night. Her life did an amazing turnaround, and she was ready to begin a new chapter.

"You've got great color. He'll be all over you for sure," Jill said.

"You look lovely. Whatever dress you choose, you'll look divine in it." Millie placed her dish aside and poured another cup of coffee. "What are we doing today?"

"We still haven't been to Universal Studios Hollywood. It's got a couple of new features, and we absolutely have to check it out. We can make arrangements downstairs." Sadie wanted to organize activities that her friends agreed upon. So far the girls let her lead the way. She'd studied the guides for weeks while she was receiving treatment. "Are you with me?"

"It sounds great." Jill pushed away from the table, stood, and went over to her side of the closet and pushed aside a few outfits. "Decisions, decisions."

"Hey, Jill. It looks like today is going to be a scorcher." Sadie pointed to the television as the weather lady was doing her report. "I'm wearing white shorts and a pink tank. No dresses for me today." She moved her hair off her forehead. "Maybe even a slicked back hairdo."

"You've become the fashionista of the group." Jill stretched out on the bed.

"Come on, LA awaits." Sadie went over and tapped the side of Jill's leg. "Aren't you going to get ready?"

"Yeah, yeah, yeah. I've been calling Tommy all morning. He's not answering. I'm supposed to be the aloof one."

Sadie sat on the edge of the bed. "I'm sure he'll call. Maybe he was sleeping. There is a three hour difference, you know."

Jill put her hand on the side of her face. "What was I thinking? He must think I'm a lunatic." She burst out laughing. "I forgot all about the time." She got up and hightailed it into the bathroom.

Millie stood in front of the mirror and fussed with her hair. "I'm putting my hair in a ponytail. Do you have any pretty hair ties?"

"Let me check." Sadie went to her side of the double closet in the hallway and lifted her smaller bag with accessories. She brought it over to the bed, opened it, and sat. "Here are a couple of different types." She handed them to her friend.

"Thanks. I'm going to miss the perks of staying with friends when we get back home. I wish we could stay longer," Millie admitted as she played with her hair.

"I know. We have to go away more often. I'm having so much fun, but I have to admit, I'm looking forward to my date on Sunday." She fumbled with a packet of rubber bands, knowing all too well how badly she wanted to feel Vince's lips on hers, to feel his strong hands on her skin, and to spend the night wrapped in his loving embrace.

Millie turned to face her. "You seem nervous. Is something bothering you?"

Sadie's gaze fell to the floor. "I'm okay. I miss

Vince already. I'm in trouble, right?" She gave a half-smile.

"No, you're not. You're in luck. I wish I could say the same about my lame relationship." Millie placed her hand on top of hers. "We all want to find that someone we can be ourselves with, and vice versa."

"You're right," Sadie replied with her voice low.

"Is there something else you're not telling me? You know you can trust me."

She gave a quick shrug and sighed. "It's my own self-doubt about my career choice. I haven't given much thought to my acting career and how much I wanted it. I sort of let it go when I decided to teach."

"Go on." Millie sat beside her. "Why are you doubting your decision now? It seems like there is more to the story."

"Vince never gave up his dream. I buckled when the going got tough. That's all. Meeting him after all these years forced me to remember the way I used to be, and the times we had together talking about our goals." It was hard to face her doubts head-on. The easy way worked better.

It had all come flooding back once she came face to face with the man who she shared her dreams with. She felt like such a hypocrite after making a vow to live her life differently after her cancer treatment had ended. *Seize the moment and have no regrets* was what she had told herself. Why was she doubting herself? Her heart was in the theater, however, she did love her students. They needed her, and she needed them.

"I think Jill is finished in there. I don't want to put a damper on the day." She waved her hand in the air and put one finger to her lips. She'd rather not prompt a group discussion about her doubts. Today was about having fun and exploring new things. "Thanks for listening." Thank goodness her besties were always there to hear her out and not judge. Things always seemed a little better after a venting session to a dear and trusted friend.

"You're welcome. You'd do the same for me." Millie gave her a quick hug, got up, and went back to the mirror. "We're going to have a marvelous day."

"Tonight we can eat at another fancy restaurant. I'll make reservations for the place with the great view in the hotel. We deserve to dine in style," Sadie insisted as she got up and strolled over to the end table to pick up her bag.

"Did I miss anything?" Jill stood in the hall with her hand on her hip, modeling a yellow sleeveless jumpsuit and a large-brimmed white hat. "Do I look like a movie star or what?"

"Yes. Next thing you know you'll have your own reality show." Sadie chucked.

"I'm ready," Millie announced as she gave Jill a once-over. "Love your outfits."

The girls left and made their way down the hall like they owned the place, with their heads up, shoulders back, and tummies tucked. Out in front of the hotel, they hopped in the van that waited to take them to Universal. The driver did a quick head count and explained about the pick-up time before he took off.

Sadie couldn't wait to enter the gates of the park. It was definitely a must-see in LA. The fun times of sightseeing in a magnificent city weren't over yet, but in a couple of days she'd be back in New Jersey to begin the next chapter in her life. Hopefully, she'd find a way to accept her decision to give up her dreams of being on the stage and appreciate the path she'd chosen instead.

"Let's take a ride in one of those trolleys that take you around the movie sets," Jill said as she popped a piece of gum into her mouth.

"I'm all for it. How about you, Millie?"

"Why not? It sounds like fun. Later on, I'd love to take a stroll on Venice Beach. The atmosphere is so Bohemian."

"I don't know what got into you, but I love the new you." Jill put her hand out and gave Millie's a friendly slap.

The mini-van stopped and the driver jumped out to open the back door. The friends got out and filed in a line to get inside the park. Sadie swayed back and forth as excited as a kid in an amusement park.

"I don't remember when I had such a fabulous time. I wonder if Vince was ever here," Sadie said.

"I knew it," Jill said as she gave Sadie a light tap on her arm.

"You knew what?" Sadie paid for the tickets.

"That you were falling hard for Mr. Good Looking."

"I'll tell him you have a new name for him." She laughed.

Sadie's sandal popped opened, and when she stopped to fasten it, her phone almost fell out of her bag. She caught it just in time. When she slipped it back into her purse, a photo of Vince appeared on the screen. It was a selfie standing in front of a theater in the city.

A knot formed in her gut. Why did she feel so uncomfortable all of a sudden? Her biggest concern was if he had to travel to LA for the pilot, not the show on Broadway. He'd be able to stay nearby if he got the part in the play. Then why did she wish he'd do the television show instead? Was she secretly envious of Vince achieving what she'd left behind?

A revolving globe was the center of attention and they stopped to get a better look. Sadie was in awe of the amazing design. She wobbled when she strained her neck to get a full view, and then she planted her feet firmly on the ground. *Steady, girl.* It took a few minutes to center herself and get a grip on her emotions.

She wasn't about to let envy stand in the way. Her uneasiness over Vince and the theater wasn't due to his talent; it was her lack of it that gnawed at her. He deserved a chance. Sadie shook off her sullen mood and trudged onward.

A grand arch led the way to a magical experience. Crowds filled the streets. Colors and light flickered all around. The sound of laughter came from all angles. People young and old had the same idea in mind on a beautiful late spring day.

"I know I sound like a dork, but can we visit the world of Harry Potter?" Sadie politely asked.

"We sure can. We're off to see the wizard." Jill's voice was high-pitched, and she sounded like she'd entered her second childhood.

With a happy smile on her face, Sadie and her friends began an adventure they'd never forget. Sadie planned on capturing the day's activities with lots of pictures and she'd show them all to Vince. They'd be home in a few days, and she'd be in Vince's arms once again.

****

Kathleen Ann Gallagher

Sadie jumped out of bed. "Hurry, we don't want to miss our plane." She'd sleep on the plane so she would look her best when Vince picked her up the following evening.

"I don't want to go home." Jill dragged herself out of bed.

"I'm with you," Millie announced as she stuck her head out of the bathroom door.

"Let me in there," Sadie said.

"I'll be out in a few. You light a fire under slowpoke Jill." Millie smiled and shut the door.

Sadie held her arms out and spun around like a dancer. "I'll never forget this magnificent vacation." She threw on a pair of tights and a comfortable pink fleece top, stuffed the last item inside her suitcase, and closed it. "You better hurry if we're going to make it to the airport on time." She reached out to give Jill her hand.

"I'll be ready. Don't worry. I showered and packed last night. Remember?"

"Oh yeah." Sadie shrugged.

"You were on the phone with Lover Boy. You two are so cute."

Millie came out of the bathroom and picked up her shoulder bag and placed it next to her suitcase on the floor. "I'm ready to go."

Jill got it together as if she was running on caffeine. She raced around to get dressed. "I'm a pro at getting ready on a minute's notice," Jill bragged.

"I'll be ready in a minute." Sadie went into the bathroom. In a few minutes, she was done. "Well, this is it. Come on, girls. Let's get out of here. New adventures await us." She went over to the window and snuck one last look at the magnificent view, then waved at the Hollywood sign. "See you again one day."

Chapter 7

"I can't believe I'm hearing the words. I'm listening, yet I have to hear you say it over again." Vince gripped the phone and shouted, waving his free arm in the air.

It was hard to wrap his head around the news. His pulse sped up and his heart thumped. What a great feeling to have validation for the craft he loved. He couldn't think of a career more suited for him. It all began as a child when he'd caught the bug to entertain, thanks to his mother, who had signed him up for a children's theater group. She'd noticed how well he performed when he was in the talent show in school, and then one night she heard him singing in the tub and hurried to drag his father in to hear. At the time, Vince didn't realize there was anything special about his abilities. It was all for fun.

"Believe it. You've earned it. Man, you've worked your ass off for it. Go out and celebrate," Joey insisted with his authoritative tone. "I heard back from the producers of *The Mall People*, and it's a no-go, so thank your lucky stars for this break, kid. They liked the premise, but it didn't fit in this season. That's how it rolls in the business."

"I couldn't ask for better timing. Sadie and I have reservations for the finest restaurant in Monmouth County for Sunday night. Now we've got something incredible to celebrate. Wait until I tell her." Vince wanted to scream it to the world.

Deep inside, he felt a twinge of disappointment over the television show, nevertheless, Broadway was his first love. *I got the part!* The four words he'd wanted to say for so long were true, and it felt amazing. A lead role in a Broadway show and the chance to work with an established actress who'd won a Tony took time to absorb.

After he'd thanked Joey a zillion times, he hung up and placed his phone on the arm of the couch. Vince needed to take a minute to gather his thoughts. With his feet up on the old chest he used for a coffee table, Vince placed his hands in back of his neck and rested his head on the couch. While he stared up at the ceiling, his heart practically leaped out of his chest. He never wanted to forget this moment. Years of sacrifice were all worth it. He'd try his best to stay humble, work hard, and never take a job for granted.

The conversation twirled around in his mind, until it sunk in. Rehearsals would start soon, and he could hardly wait. Good thing he'd kept in shape and up to date with his dance steps. A regular workout plan and proper nutrition had given him extra stamina. Like his grandmother had assured him, *good things come when you work hard*.

In a few hours he'd be able to look into Sadie's eyes, touch her silky hair, and all would be well in the world. He yearned to hold her close and bury his head on her chest, inhaling the sexy scent of her perfume. He'd already picked up his tan dress pants from the dry cleaners, along with his light blue shirt. Looking his best was a must for tonight. Maybe he'd even wear a tie. A fine bottle of champagne was needed for this occasion.

He closed his eyes and envisioned Sadie cradled in his arms. A few days apart made him want her more. He'd pledge to stay by her side. If she felt the same way, he'd do everything in his power to make her happy. He'd cherish each moment together and never let anything come between them. Vince wanted to shield her from all the evil in the world, if it was at all possible. She deserved a good life filled with the best of everything. For God's sake, she was the only woman he'd ever wanted. Sadie was a beautiful and tempting woman, and he was at her command. A magical spell fell over him when she entered a room. It wasn't like anything he'd read or seen in a movie. The feeling was unexplainable and impossible to resist.

He stood and decided to get some fresh air. Lack of sleep the previous night had started to affect him. After he yawned through a conversation with one of his neighbors on the front porch, Vince apologized and realized he needed a power nap. He'd stayed up later than usual after he'd spoken to Sadie when she'd arrived home last night.

Vince headed back inside. He pulled down the darkening shades in his studio and set his alarm to wake him in an hour and a half. The last thing he wanted was to be late to pick up Sadie. She lived in the other end of town, closer to the bay, and he couldn't wait to see her house. Once his head hit the pillow, his whole body relaxed, and he heard himself snore before he zonked out.

****

Now that she'd unpacked and organized her

weekly planner, Sadie brewed a cup of ginger-peach tea, carried it out to the patio, and set it down on the table. She cranked open the red umbrella and sat. It was late May, and her garden had grown in a week's time. Mr. Martin, her retired neighbor, had been nice enough to agree to water her flowers and grass while she was gone. Maybe next year she'd have a sprinkler installed. The fragrance from the annuals drifted her way. She inhaled the sweet scent as she sipped her tea. What a glorious day.

It was like a bird sanctuary in her backyard with all of the trees and the singing species. She'd gotten a nice tan, and with a seasonably warm day, she'd be able to wear one of her new dresses tonight. She put her legs up on another chair and took a deep breath. In a few hours, she'd be with Vince, and it was hard to believe they'd found each other in LA.

Her trip to California was embedded deep in her memory and she couldn't wait to print the photos. There were even a couple of pictures of Vince in the batch. Jill had snapped them at the after-party. You could always count on her to capture memorable events. Sadie was glad to have a photo of their unofficial first date.

Luckily, Sadie didn't have to go back to work until Monday, and then tryouts would begin soon after. The principal had been so understanding during her disability leave. She looked forward to being back with her students. They'd kept in touch during her treatment and sent cards, homemade cookies, and flowers. It touched her heart to receive their love and support.

The tea had warmed her insides and helped her relax. Sadie savored the last drop. Her heart fluttered and her hands trembled as it got closer to the moment she'd gaze into Vince's smoldering eyes. She gathered the cup and coaster before heading back inside.

Once she rinsed the few things in the sink, she went upstairs to start getting ready. There was plenty of time, but it was best to be done early. A slow, steady whirlwind started in her belly as she scurried around her room. She bent over and straighten her lavender chenille bedspread and fluffed a pillow.

Vince might be beside her in her bed soon, if all went well. She imagined his bare chest up against her breasts as she ran her tongue along his neck moving toward his tempting lips. In the past, she'd never admit to wanting a man sexually. But things were different now. She'd realized that life didn't wait for anyone. If Vince read her mind, they might not make it through dinner. It wasn't a regular occurrence to bring a man home, but this wasn't just any man. He was someone she'd fallen deeply for many years ago. Her foolishness and hang-ups held her back. This time she'd hold on tight and never let go.

It was time to get ready. She undressed and went into the bathroom. Just as she was about to get into the tub, her phone rang. She'd left it on the nightstand, so she grabbed a bath towel and ran out to answer it.

"You're out of breath. I'm sorry to make you run," Jill said.

"No problem. How's it going?" Sadie held her towel around her and shivered. She went over to the switch next to the door and turned off the fan.

"I need another week off work. I didn't get much sleep. Tommy must have missed me, because he's acting like a romantic fool," she said in a low tone.

"Is he listening?"

"No, I'm just tired."

"Well, isn't that a good thing?" Sadie laughed.

"Enough about my life. I'll tell you when we have more time to chat. I called to wish you luck tonight with your man. I hope you have a fantastic night."

"Me too. Thank you for calling. I'll tell him you said hi." Sadie started toward the bathroom.

"I'm so happy for you."

"Go get some rest. Your voice is cracking."

As soon as Sadie finished her bubble bath, she wrapped herself in a soft, white terrycloth towel and piled her hair up in a smaller one. She turned the extra-bright light on next to the mirror and used an exfoliating face wash. The cucumber scent was refreshing. Once it was time to rinse, she splashed warm water on her face and ran her hand over her cheeks, happy she didn't have a last minute breakout. Her skin glowed. Sadie used a new toothpaste along with a whitening gel. She'd tried it while she was on vacation, and it surprised her when it worked. A luscious lavender-scented body cream made her legs feel like silk. If she hurried, she'd have time to light a couple of candles and put on her favorite instrumental CD to set the mood for the evening.

It took a few minutes in front of her closet to decide if she'd wear the black dress or the floral print. She'd purchased both since she couldn't make up her mind. Since Vince was taking her to a fine dining restaurant, she went with the sleeveless black one. It had gold trim around a sexy V-neck, but it wasn't too revealing. Just enough to keep him intrigued. A touch of stitching in the midriff added a nice effect. With a dainty vintage necklace, matching earrings, and strappy black sandals, she'd be sure to look her best.

Sadie slipped into her dress and sat on the bed. She fastened her sandals, and then she went over to her vanity and applied the finishing touches. Her hands shook slightly as she put on her mascara and added a pretty shade of glittery, pink lip-gloss. Hopefully, once Vince put his arms around her, she'd calm down.

Sadie stood in front of the full-length mirror in her room and took once last look at herself. She turned from side to side, admiring her dress. After she picked up her beaded clutch bag, she went downstairs. Tonight was the ideal time to light the mulled wine scented candle she'd received as a gift from one of her students last Christmas. She placed the decorative jar on the coffee table, lit it, and moved over to the stereo and popped in the soundtrack to *Out of Africa*. She'd watched the movie with her mother and found the music along with the cinematography beautiful.

When her phone rang, she lowered the music. "Hello, Mom. I'm about to go out on a date," Sadie announced.

"I was calling to ask how your trip went. I'm sorry to call at a bad time."

"That's okay, Mom. I'll fill you in tomorrow." She ran her hand across the back of her hair. "Will you be home in the afternoon?" She paced around the room, anticipating Vince's arrival.

She was grateful her mother already liked Vince, and she anticipated she'd be happy to hear they were dating. A couple of times, when they were teenagers, Sadie had invited Vince and a few of the other members of the cast over her house, and it was usually awkward.

Her mother always thought Vince had a crush on her, yet he didn't do a thing about it. She guessed Mom had been right. She smiled at the thought.

Funny how Mrs. De Carlo and her mom were already friends. They knew each other from various functions in town and had worked on committees for a charity together. It should be interesting to hear her mother's reaction.

"I plan on going to the beach in the morning to take some photos, but I'll be home early. I can't wait to hear how it went. I love you. You deserve happiness, honey. Remember you come first," her mother said before they hung up.

She knew her mom was onto her about her sadness over leaving her acting career in the wings. Many times she tried to encourage her to go for the career she was passionate about. Sadie told herself that teaching was her passion, but now she had serious doubts.

Sadie rested one knee on the sofa and peeked out the living room window. When she stood and turned to grab her compact from her purse, she heard the sound of tires on the gravel in her driveway and a door slam. Her insides rattled as she waited for Vince to ring the bell. It wasn't a good idea to appear overly eager. Jill and Millie had given her tips on how to keep a man interested, and the first one was to keep him on his toes. They didn't have the best relationships, but she knew their hearts were in the right place.

Vince rang the doorbell, and Sadie opened the door. Her heart leaped into her throat when he smiled and handed her a beautiful bouquet of brightly colored flowers. She welcomed him inside and he leaned down and gave her a gentle, yet passion-filled kiss on the lips.

For a second, she felt like she'd been swept away to a far-off place. Vince did that to her. One touch and she was gone. She steadied herself. Somehow she knew he wouldn't show up without a token of his affection. The Vince she'd kept in her heart was a hopeless romantic. She was happy he hadn't changed. He'd only gotten better with age.

"You have no idea how happy I am to see you. It seems like we've been apart for ages," he said with a sincerity in his voice that warmed her heart. Vince followed her when she took the flowers into the kitchen. "Do you need help with those?"

"I'm good." She gave him a playful grin. "I've got the perfect pink crystal vase tucked under the sink." She bent down to get it and sensed Vince watching her every move.

Sadie moved over to the counter and took a knife from a holder and carefully cut the stems, filled the vase with water, and arranged the beautiful selection of flowers.

"I'll carry that for you." Vince politely took the vase from her hands.

"I think they'll look pretty on the dining room table." She led the way.

Vince carried the vase into the dining room and set it down on the table. A sense of excitement made her feel like a girl on the way to her first dance. Her emotions were in charge of her mind. Sadie took a deep breath.

"You have a great place here. Did you hire an interior decorator?" Vince asked.

"I wish. I got the ideas from some of my favorite design magazines. With a touch of whimsy, I created my own style."

"It shows your personality and reflects your artistic flair."

Her heart pitter-pattered when Vince stood close. "Thank you."

He possessed all of the qualities she'd ever wanted in a man. She'd told herself all chances of a romance with him were lost, since they hadn't kept in touch, but as soon as she laid eyes on him standing in the lobby in LA, her blood sizzled through her veins.

"I'd love to stay here and have an intimate dinner for two, but we've got reservations," Vince whispered close to her ear.

"So would I, but we can come back here later."

Vince's eyes held a sexy stare as he slipped his arm around her. He bent over and kissed her neck, sending an electrical current right down to her fingertips. She rested her head on his shoulder for a moment, feeling special, and then she stepped back. If they didn't leave now, they'd never make it to the restaurant on time.

"I'll get my things." She couldn't wait to curl up beside him in bed and make up for the time they'd spent apart. Sadie went into the kitchen, picked up her clutch from the counter, and reached inside to take her keys out. "I'm ready."

Her heart nearly jumped out of her chest when she turned and found him staring at her, arms crossed with one hand on his chin, as if he was admiring a beautiful painting. The intensity in his gorgeous blue eyes almost made her stop and undress him in the foyer, but she'd wait. She had to force herself to keep it together. All it took was a look and she was all his. Sadie sucked in her stomach and held her head high as they left her place.

They strolled down her walkway side by side, and as her hand brushed up against his, Sadie wanted to take hold of it, but she held back. It might be better to let him take charge.

Vince held the car door open while Sadie got in and buckled up. She placed her hand across the soft leather seats. He'd kept the older model in excellent shape. She ran her tongue along her lips with thoughts of after dinner creeping into her head. Sadie tried to focus on the moment, however, she craved his lips and his hands all over her body. The romantic phase had begun, and she was enjoying every minute of it.

"I've got so much to tell you," Vince said.

"I'm all ears." The excitement in his tone piqued her interest.

"I was going to give you an exclusive during dinner, but I can't wait," he openly confessed.

"What is it, Vince?" What did he have up his sleeve? Was he about to announce they'd have to hold off on getting too serious due to him traveling to LA to set up temporary housing? She fidgeted in her seat, her stomach in knots.

Before he pulled out, Vince blurted, "I scored the role as the lead in the Broadway show I auditioned for." His eyes twinkled like a kid about to blow out his birthday candles.

"You what?" She couldn't help but raise her voice as she put her hand over her mouth. He'd waited his whole life for this opportunity. "Wow, you're kidding? I'm so happy for you. I knew you'd get a break sooner or later. You're too talented not to." Her words flowed as she struggled to keep her own insecurities tucked away.

It was only right to celebrate. She had made the choice to leave the business and pursue other avenues. If she had her doubts, it was her own fault. This was not the time to voice her deepest regrets. She put on a smile and reached over to touch his shoulder. Sadie ran her hand gently along his arm. He backed out and they were on their way.

Once they'd stopped at a red light in Spring Lake, Vince turned and placed his lips on hers. "I can't get enough of you," he admitted. His fingers laced through hers helped stop the clattering in her head.

When the light changed, Vince put his hands back on the wheel, and Sadie glanced out at the stately homes along the water. "It must be nice to wake up to a view like this every morning."

"No matter where I travel, The Jersey Shore will always be the place for me. There's something I can't explain here. Maybe it's because I spent my childhood with visions of the boardwalk in my head as I went to sleep at night." He laughed. "Sorry I sound overly nostalgic."

"I'm with you. It is a beautiful evening." Sadie inhaled the sea air, wishing the night would never end.

She tried to focus on Vince's good fortune instead of her regrets. Since they'd reconnected, all types of scenarios flooded her mind. She'd even pictured them strolling barefoot, hand and hand on the beach as they confessed their love for one another. Maybe she'd watched too many romantic movies lately, or maybe it was time to fall in love and it was all part of the process. Whatever her future held, Vince definitely had a place in it.

"What about the television show? Have you heard

anything?" Sadie was curious how he'd juggle both.

"It's funny." He gave a lighthearted chuckle. "You know how they say when one door closes another one opens? The show didn't get picked up for the fall season. I'm back where I belong, on the stage."

Since he had such a huge smile on his face, she'd let it rest. She wasn't about to divulge her insecurities over leaving the theater. He deserved to bask in his glory, not pity her for lost opportunities. It was her own fault. How she'd love to go back in time.

Vince pulled into the parking lot of the restaurant, shut off the car, and turned to face her. "It is a miracle to have found you again at this time in my life." He took Sadie's hand in his own. "I couldn't be happier."

"I feel the same way." She held his gaze as her heart melted.

Vince hopped out and ran around to open the car door. She took his hand and stepped out onto the pavement, looked up at the sky, and thanked her lucky stars for this gift of love.

Once they were inside, a pleasant young woman dressed in a pale yellow, sleeveless dress escorted them to a corner table. There was just enough sunlight filtering in to set the mood for a romantic evening. Gold wall sconces, white linen tablecloths, and dainty pink flowers displayed in a crystal vase sat on each table. The soft sound of piano music played in the background. They were seated and handed an elegant red leather menu.

"I haven't been here in years." Sadie opened her napkin and placed it on her lap.

She glanced over the selections. Vince rested his arm on the table and reached over to caress her hand.

Sadie didn't know how much more attention she could take before she could no longer contain her emotions. All she wanted was to be alone with him. Her spicy thoughts wouldn't quit.

"I've been here a few times over the last couple of years, but a business dinner can't come close to spending time with you," he said, never taking his eyes off her. "Do you remember when we had a party to celebrate opening night here?"

"Oh yeah. That was the night Marty proposed to Michelle. She delivered her lines in a trance throughout the whole show. We got the best reviews that night." Sadie laughed.

"It seems like yesterday," he added.

"I know. I can't believe it's been ten years since we've performed together."

She'd never forgotten the sultry look in Vince's eyes when he delivered his lines in their love scenes. Somehow she'd always known he was the one for her, even though he didn't confess his feelings back then. Chemistry can't be denied. It's all in the timing, and the LA reunion was a blessing. She took a deep breath. If only she'd be able to keep her promise and let go of the recurring thoughts of giving up her own acting career. Her eyes welled up. *Why won't these feelings quit?*

"Is something wrong?" Vince gave her a concerned look. He knew her all too well.

"I'm fine, and happy to be here with you."

She'd better watch herself or he'd never give up on asking her about it. He'd always been able to read her mind. She'd almost forgotten how well. Sadie put on a smile.

"The new chef is even better than the one who

opened the place. His specialty is seafood."

"Great. I'm in the mood for shrimp," she said as she scanned the seafood entrée section.

Once the waiter took their orders and poured a couple of glasses of white wine, Sadie was able to relax. After a delectable meal, she checked out the dessert menu.

All through coffee and dessert, they reminisced about the fun times they'd shared back in the day. Sadie felt the light brush of his leg under the table. An electric surge shot up her skirt, and she pressed her legs together while a shiver swept across her. He knew exactly what he was doing to her. After he paid the check, they walked outside to find the sky filled with stars, and the sea breeze made her skin tingle.

"It's a nice night for a stroll on the boardwalk." Vince stopped on the porch and placed his hands on the railing. "How about it?"

"I'd love it."

Vince grabbed her hand, his touch gentle, and they headed to the beach. He took on a long stride, and she kept up with his pace. "If I didn't step out of my comfort zone, I would have missed out on a splendid night like this."

The sweet scent of honeysuckle lingered in the air, and the deep blue sky turned shades of red. As they got closer to the boardwalk, she had flashbacks of when they were younger and used to gather after rehearsals, start a bonfire, and roast marshmallows on the beach. That was if the police didn't catch them. All they had wanted was to have some harmless fun, yet most of the time they'd have to put out the fire. Vince had serenaded her with his guitar on a summer night after the final reading, and she had hoped he'd lean in and steal a real-life kiss, unlike the scripted one they'd done minutes before on the stage, but he didn't. It had seemed better to tuck the memories away in a safe place and leave the past alone. She had figured that he'd moved on by now. It seemed unimaginable that a great guy like Vince was still unattached.

"It's so beautiful here. I'd love to be able to live so close to the water. Maybe one day." She shrugged.

"You might just find yourself getting your wish. My buddy works as a realtor, and sometimes a great house goes on the market for an affordable price, especially if they want a quick sale," he said, his tone soft.

"Is something wrong?" she asked.

"No, I'm fantastic. How could I be anything else while spending time with you?" He gave her hand a gentle squeeze.

Why wasn't she convinced?

They stood at the light on Ocean Avenue and waited. Vince placed his arm around her shoulder and she nestled close. The woodsy scent of his cologne tempted her. She looked up at him, and he brushed the side of her face as if she was a found treasure.

It felt wonderful to feel desirable again. When her hair had thinned during her treatment and her eyelashes fell out, she'd stared in the mirror, wondering if she'd ever be her old self again. Now, she felt vibrant and alive. Every touch of Vince's hand sent a rush of heat through her from the top of her head down to her toes.

"Those kids remind me of us." She nodded toward the shore. A couple of teenagers gathered near the entrance to the beach. Sadie slipped her arm through

Vince's and gave a soft sigh.

"Yeah, I see what you mean. We had some great times, and I'm ready to build new memories with you, Sadie." He stopped and turned to face her. "Do I sound like a Hallmark card?" He gave her an adoring grin.

"No way. It was sweet of you to say." She smiled. "I mean it."

Vince shared his feelings the way she'd always dreamed he would. He was one sexy dude, and she was floating on air.

He guided her to the railing next to the beach, and they stared out at the ocean. It held a mystery in the evening hours, with the sound of the gulls over the water's edge. The soothing scent reminded Sadie of summer fun.

Vince turned to face her, gently lifting her chin, and then he took her in his arms and planted his lips softly against hers. He dipped his tongue in and out of her mouth while Sadie's head spun. She was up in the clouds and falling hard for this wonderful man.

Chapter 8

Vince wasn't about to mess this up. Every grain of his being wanted to swoop Sadie up into his arms and carry her home to make mad love to her, but his gut instinct told him to hold back. This wasn't all about sex.

He shifted back and forth while his palms got sweaty and his eye started to twitch. Sadie was the sweetest woman he'd even known. But his financial situation wouldn't allow him to treat her like he wanted. He wasn't able to take her on more romantic dinners or a weekend getaway; even a movie this week would set him back. He'd borrowed more than enough from his mother, and he wasn't about to ask for more.

All he needed was a little time to devote to the upcoming Broadway show, and to earn a decent paycheck. He hung his head with guilt tearing at his heart. He'd do what he had to do to make it, before he lost her again. He was proud of his work and the multiple possibilities he had in the future.

"A penny for your thoughts," Sadie said.

"My grandma used to say that." He laughed.

Sadie smiled. "So did mine." She tilted her head. "Well?"

"I was thinking how great it feels to be here with you."

"That's sweet. Thank you. I'm happy to be here with you too."

"Let's sit here and wait for the sunset." He motioned to a bench. Vince would give it his best effort to enjoy the rest of the evening with this amazing woman. She was worth waiting for.

"That's a wonderful idea. It's going to be a spectacular one. The sky is already pink." Sadie gave a cute little grin. She beat him to the bench and sat.

He sat next to her. "Come over here." Vince pulled her close, placed his arm around her, and felt like all was well in the world.

His heart thumped hard when she laid her head on his shoulder and placed her delicate hand on his chest. He had to bite his lip to keep from weakening. Maybe if the show did well, then he'd move forward with a class act like Sadie. It broke him in two to let her down, however, his decision to take her home after their evening at the beach was made. The least he could do was offer to stop for an ice cream before he make an excuse about getting to bed early due to his schedule. Hopefully, she'd understand. Sadie was always thoughtful and understanding. His mind filled with reasons why he should leave his fears behind and go for it, yet his pride took hold of his emotions. In his gut, he knew he was doing the right thing.

"I could stay here with you forever," Sadie confessed.

"Forever isn't long enough, my sweet Sadie."

"There's no place I'd rather be." Her sexy tone close to his ear made it difficult for him to think straight.

He ran his fingers across her silky hair, and he swallowed hard. She lifted her head and stared at him with a gleam in her eye that reached in and took hold of his heart. He must have done something right to deserve the affection and attention of a woman so precious.

"Why don't we hurry down to the water and get our feet wet? There's a few minutes to spare before the sun sets. We can snap a picture from the shoreline as the sun sets in back of us." Sadie stood.

"Okay. Let's go." He hurried to take off his shoes and socks and toss them aside.

Sadie did the same, and they began a slow jog. She gave him a playful pat on the butt as he took the lead.

"I'll get you back." He started a slow chase as she jolted ahead of him.

The sand kicked up as he ran with the sound of Sadie's laughter making him want her more. Vince caught hold of her at the water's edge, and he twirled her around. They both laughed aloud.

He held her close and put his hands on the sides of her face. "You look radiant tonight." He gazed deep into her eyes.

She made the move to kiss him this time. Sadie put her arms around his neck, went up on her tiptoes, and placed her lips on his. With their bodies pressed together, Vince almost gave up his plan to take it slow until he could afford to treat her right.

"Let's get ready, the sun is about to go down," Sadie said while she got her phone out of her crossover purse.

They stood with their backs to the water and put their heads together.

"Smile," she said as she snapped a photo. She captured a few more shots and showed him the pictures. "I can send them to you if you'd like."

"The first one of us as a couple. Hopefully, the first

of many. This way I can see your smile first thing in the morning, and I can't think of a better way to start the day," he admitted.

"You flatter me. Even if you're fibbing," Sadie said.

"Why don't you believe me? I'm crazy about you. I always have been."

"Really?" She pushed her hair out of her eyes.

"Yes. Can't you tell?"

"If you say so," she teased and crossed her arms.

"Are you cold?"

"It's getting a little cool." Sadie shivered.

Vince wrapped his arms around her.

"I'm nice and warm now." She looked up at him and gave a seductive grin.

"Let's head back." Vince took her hand.

They turned and headed to the spot they'd taken off their shoes.

He let go of her hand and picked up both pairs. "Are you ready?" he asked.

"It's so peaceful on the beach at night, but I'm ready."

Vince had every intention of spending plenty of nights on the beach with her. In due time. Now the hard part. He'd have to drive her home and say goodnight. He wasn't telling a lie. An early morning meeting at the theater was scheduled. His stomach twisted, yet he'd stick to the plan.

They walked to the car and Vince held the passenger side door open as Sadie got in. He turned on the radio before he took off. On the drive home, Sadie was talkative. Vince nodded and listened as she shared a few details about her upcoming class auditions, all the time wishing she'd be next to him in bed when he woke up in the morning.

She definitely was not the kind of woman to take lightly. Their relationship needed nurturing, and he needed money to take her to all the places he wanted to. A sleepover wouldn't be the way to go tonight. His rent was due and he needed to pay the car insurance next week. He'd be driving into the city for rehearsals, and he had to buy new tires for his old relic of a car. At least he'd kept it in good shape. Sadie seemed to like it.

Vince turned onto her street, and she got awfully quiet. He pulled into her driveway and left the motor running.

"Aren't you coming inside?" she asked, her tone high-pitched.

He took a deep breath, turned to face her, and reached for her hand. "I'd love to, but I've got to get up bright and early to go into the city. A meeting with the cast. It's mandatory. I'm sorry." His whole mood had shifted. He hoped she didn't mistake it for indifference. "I'll call you tomorrow, if that's all right with you."

"That's fine." She scrunched up her forehead and hesitated, then gave a couple of tiny nods. "Thank you for a great evening." She fumbled with her purse, and her smile turned into a frown. "Are you trying to tell me something?"

"I'm not trying to tell you anything but the truth." He kept his tone even. "I'm sorry. I'll make it up to you. I promise."

Vince had hoped she'd understand, and maybe even be agreeable, since tomorrow was a work day. With a forced smile on his face, he gave her a long, hard stare and at the same time he tried to keep his cool.

When he leaned over and reached for her, she pulled away at first.

"Come on, Sadie. We're not kids anymore. You've got to know you're the only woman for me."

Sadie glanced down before she finally softened and responded to his touch. He cushioned her in an embrace, and as he kissed her, she reached down and massaged his thigh. Before it got too hot, he managed to divert her affections, and he placed his forehead on top of hers. With a soft flick of his lips, he kissed her head.

"I'll walk you to the door." He turned off the car and got out.

She opened her own door and waited. Vince took her hand and walked her to her doorstep.

"Get a good night's sleep and I'll talk to you tomorrow." He smiled and turned back one more time before he made it down the walkway.

Sadie smiled and waved as she stood inside her foyer.

****

Sadie had no idea what went wrong. They'd already made love, but now that they were back in town... What was going on? She wanted to believe him about an early meeting. Why was it she didn't? Her intuition was usually right. Maybe he had a girlfriend to contend with. Her fears multiplied as she peeled off her clothes and went into the bathroom to wash her face. She used a peach-scented facial scrub and rubbed her skin hard, trying to figure him out.

He could have made his meeting if he'd stayed the night. Instead, the beautiful night had come to a harsh ending. It was probably for the best. He'd be starting his long journey to becoming a Broadway star, and maybe even be nominated for a Tony, while she stayed in this small town and led a group of high school kids in an amateur show. What a sideswipe to the life she'd dreamed about.

She put on a pair of soft cotton pajamas and went into the kitchen to make a cup of herbal tea. It was still early enough to call Jill. She had experience in the dating world. Once the water had boiled, Sadie poured the tea and grabbed a handful of chocolate chip cookies. She needed something sweet after her big letdown. Once she had curled up in an overstuffed down-filled chair in her living room, she dialed her friend.

"Hi. Are you in bed?"

"No, I'm watching an old movie. What's wrong?"

"Oh, nothing."

"Didn't you have a date with Vince?"

"Yeah, I did."

"You're home early, aren't you? And why does it sound like you're about to cry?" Jill asked.

"I'm not going to cry. It...it's just that I'm so confused." Sadie took a deep breath.

"About what? Let me turn the television off."

"It's Vince. He's acting different." She picked up her tea and took a gulp.

"What do you mean? Does he have a girlfriend on the side? I knew it! That no good—"

"I don't think he's seeing someone else. We had a wonderful time tonight. The thing that worries me is that he didn't come inside after the date. He gave me the excuse that he had an early meeting at the theater." She sniffled.

"Well, maybe it's the truth. Although it is strange

for a man to not want a booty call. Right?"

"That's exactly right. He did seem genuinely interested though." She ran her hand along the back of her hair, feeling frustrated. Her heart pounded in her ears.

"You know he's into you. Don't worry, he must have a good reason. You make a great couple, and I saw the way he looked at you. Do you want me and Millie to come over? I can pick her up and we'll be there in less than an hour."

Her offer was sincere, and Sadie appreciated it. "I'll be okay. I feel a little better. Thanks for listening."

"Are you sure?" Jill asked.

"Yes, I'm sure. I'll talk to you soon. I've got a big day tomorrow at school. Tryouts."

"Okay. Goodnight, honey."

It was a great comfort to have friends who cared. After she finished her tea, Sadie got up, turned off the lights, double-checked the door, and went into the bedroom. She pulled down the comforter and ran her hand across the crisp, clean, designer sheets. She'd changed them with hopes Vince would spend the night. Sadie thought they'd shared something special. Her heart felt heavy, yet she tried to remind herself she was operating on emotions, not logic. He wouldn't have been as affectionate during dinner if he didn't want her too.

As she was about to get under the covers her phone rang. When she picked it up, she was surprised to find it was Vince calling. Did he change his mind?

"I wanted to say goodnight and tell you how bad I feel about having to leave you," he said. "I'm about to hop into bed, but I have you on my mind."

"Me too," she responded. "I understand." She wasn't about to let on how disappointed she was.

"You have no idea how good it is to hear that you understand. I wouldn't have gone home if I didn't have so much going on."

"No problem. Good luck tomorrow."

"Thanks. I hope you have a good turnout for the auditions."

She had worried for no reason. Sadie shrugged and grabbed a book from the drawer in her nightstand before she crawled into bed. With a couple of pillows behind her back, she adjusted the clip-on light she'd received from her mother at Christmas. Reading might stop her from wishing she was going along with Vince to the theater and about to begin a promising career on the stage.

She didn't realize she'd chosen an old book by Danielle Steele. Oh, well. Anything would do right now. Even a book she might have read before would work. As long as she got lost in the story.

She usually enjoyed a love story, but not tonight. It turned out to be a bad idea to read a romance. Her chest tightened as it got to the love scene. She tossed the book to the side and pulled the covers over her head. Sadie curled up on her side and the tears slowly started to fall.

****

Vince jumped up when his alarm sounded, and he quickly decided to skip his morning jog. He yawned and dragged himself into the shower. After he brushed his teeth, shaved, and got dressed, he went to the kitchen and prepared a protein shake. He wasn't in the mood for anything else. As he poured his drink, he combed his hair back. He couldn't get Sadie off his mind. The image of the disappointed look in her eyes when he'd dropped her off stayed with him.

Before he left to catch the train, he double-checked the schedule on his phone. There was plenty of time. The traffic wasn't bad in town, so he made it to the station in less than ten minutes. Once he parked, Vince started toward the platform. He'd purchase his ticket inside the train.

He proceeded with his head in the clouds, but stopped short when he saw his father sitting on a bench. Not today. He took a few deep breaths and decided not to ruin his day by showing resentment. He'd promised his mother he'd give his dad a chance.

Vince went over to the bench and sat down beside his father. "How's it going?"

His dad looked like he'd seen a ghost. His face was pale, his eyes bulged, and he stuttered. "What...what...are you doing here this early?" His hands trembled as he reached into his shirt pocket and took out a lighter.

Vince knew he wasn't drunk because there was no smell of alcohol on his breath. His dad always shook before he took his first drink of the day. "Sorry to startle you, Dad. I've got an early meeting with the members of the cast for a new show I'm set to star in."

He stared at the dark circles and lines around his father's eyes. The years of abuse he'd put his body through had taken their toll. There was a time when he had been a handsome dude. His mom always commented about how much Vince resembled his dad.

"That's right. Your mother called me and filled me in." He put his hand on Vince's shoulder. "I'm incredibly proud of you, son." He hit the bottom of a pack of cigarettes, took one out, and lit it.

There was a sincerity in his tone that was refreshing. Somehow, Vince believed him. "Thank you. You know you should stop smoking."

"Let me work on one vice at a time." He took a puff. "For a guy who just got a big break, you don't look happy. Is there something you want to talk about?"

The last person Vince thought he'd be confining in was his father, but he had to get it off of his chest. "I am a little off-balance today. You see, I think I screwed up my chance with Sadie. Do you remember the girl I used to bring to the house once in a while back in school? We were in the theater company together."

His father rubbed the top of his brow. "Oh yeah, I remember her. She was a sweet girl. You had a crush on her, didn't you?" He grinned.

"I was crazy about her, I still am, and I think she feels the same about me." Oddly enough, it felt good to share his feelings with the man he'd shunned for so long. "By the way, where are you going?"

"I have an interview," he proudly announced.

"Great. Are you ready to go back to work?" Vince wanted desperately to forget how his father's illness had robbed them of so many years, not to mention the mental anguish his mother had suffered. Deep inside, he'd hoped the day would come when they'd reconnect.

"I've got three months under my belt, and my sponsor supports me all the way. And if I get hired, I can still make meetings in the evenings." He shifted his position.

"I'm thrilled to hear good news." An overwhelming sense of relief rushed over him. He glanced up at the schedule to see if the train was on time.

"Why do you feel you lost your chance with Sadie?"

Vince took a deep breath, turned toward his father, and kept his tone low. "Long story, but I'll make it short. I took her to a nice restaurant in Spring Lake for a romantic dinner. It's one of Sadie's favorite places." Vince gave a reluctant sigh. "We had a great time, but I went way over my budget. You know I'm a waiter, and while I pursue my acting career, my finances haven't exactly been stable." Vince felt a twinge of uneasiness divulging his concerns to his father. It'd been so long since any chance of a connection was possible.

"So why do you think things went wrong? It sounds like you had a special evening. Didn't you?" He moved a little closer.

"That's where I went wrong. I split when I dropped her off, when I could have spent the night at her place." Vince put his head down and felt a gnawing in his gut. The muscles in his back tightened. "I'm not in a position to get serious."

"I'm going to tell you something I've learned, son." His tone was one of authority as he straightened his shoulders and held his head up. "You aren't in control of who you fall in love with and when it happens. It's all in His hands." He pointed up to the sky. "I want you to listen and don't interrupt me. I've managed to put together a few bucks. I didn't go through all of my inheritance like your mother might think. It was tied up for a while."

"What are you saying?" Vince sat forward and raised his voice a notch.

"I told you not to butt in. Please, hear me out. The money recently became available. I was broke a few days ago too, but now I can finally do something worthy. I'm giving you a check to cover your expenses until you get on your feet."

His father was usually a quiet man, but a transformation took place sitting on the platform. He'd used his wisdom to assist his son, instead of wallowing in self-destructive behavior.

"I can't accept a handout. You need to take care of yourself." Vince folded his hands and tried not to get overly emotional. He had to admit it felt great to get along, and it had been so long since he'd felt loved by his father; not that money was a way to show love. His heart showed in his words, and Vince appreciated his father's generosity.

"I won't take no for an answer." He stood and stared directly into Vince's eyes. "The train will be here in a minute. We can talk more about it on the ride into the city."

Vince's head throbbed the minute he stood. He rubbed the back of his neck. To his amazement, he detected a sincerity in his father's words. The rent was due, and he'd pay him back. It was about time his dad did something for his family.

"I might just take you up on your offer," Vince finally said.

His father nodded, a satisfied grin on his face. "Let's go take care of business. We both have so much to be thankful for."

****

Sadie awoke to the sound of a beautiful Spanish guitar solo on the radio. As she stretched she peeked at the clock on her nightstand. She didn't remember falling asleep, but she'd always felt better after a good cry. There was plenty of time to grab a light breakfast and get ready for work. Things made sense in the morning. Sadie had found a special man. After everything she'd been through over the past year, her emotions were all over the place. Their connection was real. There was no need for overreacting, and she was certainly not in a rush. Maybe PMS had clouded her senses. She was a little embarrassed by her behavior.

She was excited to begin auditions today. She picked up the book from her bed and was about to put it back in the drawer of her nightstand when she noticed a couple of envelopes had fallen on the floor. Strange how she didn't see them last night. From the edge of the bed, she bent over to pick them up. Sadie opened one of the folded papers and her heart leaped into her throat. She trembled as she read it. It was her acceptance letter for The Actors Studio in NYC. Only a select few get to attend the prestigious school. Why did she forfeit her chance?

She stood at her bedside, still shaking. A tear fell down her cheek, and she reached for a tissue. She wiped her face and quickly stuck the letter back in the envelope. At the time, her mind had been made up. Her mother had supported her decision, and she went on to get a teaching degree. Her calling was not in the theater. She didn't have what it took. Her skin was thin, not tough enough to take rejections, critics, and haters. So why did it hurt so badly?

Sadie fastened her robe and moved over to open the curtains. She stayed at the window for a moment. The grass was bright green and the light touch of morning dew made it glisten.

Enough of this self-pity mode. It was time to get ready. Her students needed her.

She sprinted into the bathroom, took off her pajamas, and jumped into the shower. The rain shower she recently had installed was heavenly. She lathered her body with a new body wash she'd found in a specialty shop downtown. It was invigorating. The light scent of citrus and ginger was ideal for a morning pick-me-up.

In less than fifteen minutes, she was dressed and parked on a stool at the kitchen counter with a cup of coffee, munching on an oversized cranberry-orange protein bar. She'd grab a banana and a handful of blueberries for later in the morning.

Sadie grabbed her keys from the table by the door and picked up her purse, along with her leather folder, and left for work. After a short drive, she arrived at school. The students rambled along as she headed to her classroom. Today's lesson was centered on auditioning. It was a good lead into the big event after school. As she approached her desk, a message appeared on her phone. She took a moment to read it, and it brought a smile to her face. Vince wrote that he missed her and was thinking about her. He'd been in the city for an hour, and her heart skipped a beat when she read over his words. *He couldn't get me out of his mind.*

****

The school day went well, and it was finally the big moment. Sadie was lucky to have the director of the drama department, Ms. Cartwright, by her side. A middle-aged woman who was poised and professional, she greeted the students as they filed into the auditorium.

"We have our job cut out for us." Ms. Cartwright smiled as she took a seat at the table. "There is so much talent in the group this year." She raised her brows and tapped a pencil on her coffee cup.

The auditorium had recently been remodeled and it had a nice-sized stage with two sets of wooden stairs, one on each side. A red velvet curtain made it look like a theater in NYC. Paintings of scholars were strategically placed on the walls to inspire, and brand new, large windows allowed the room natural lighting. Ultra-modern lighting was available for special functions. The seats were comfortable with extra padding. One of the wealthy townspeople had donated a huge check to remodel the school auditorium. The area hadn't been redone in over twenty years. You could still smell the fresh paint as soon as you entered the room. An area set up in the front of the stage gave them the perfect view.

An older, white-haired woman with dimples and a cackle for a laugh, who had played piano for them in the past, sat on the bench. She waved and winked when she was ready to go. "One, two, three, set to go." She laughed.

Sadie chuckled to herself.

The lights were set to center stage. It was time to begin.

The students knew the material like true professionals, and they gave it their best shot. A few of them stood out, and Sadie had them do a second audition for the lead roles. Everyone got along. There was no jealousy or disruptive behavior. She'd taught them well.

One of the girls she had her eye on sat in the corner with her head down. Her name was Marla Miles. Sadie announced a fifteen minute break and went over to speak to her.

"I thought you'd be happy to be a top contender for the lead." Sadie put her hand out in an effort to help Marla up. "Come on, let's talk."

"Thanks, Ms. Layne. I am happy. It's just that Carolyn is a much better singer and actress than I am." She looked away. "Why am I here and she didn't get a second read?" Her hands trembled.

"You're a very talented young woman. Roles are cast for multiple reasons. There was something special about the way you portrayed the character. The first and most important thing is to have faith in yourself."

Sadie's lecture to her student sounded exactly like the one she'd received from a guidance counselor when she was the same age. It was funny how things came full circle. She put her arm around Marla's shoulder.

The memory of a similar situation popped into Sadie's mind. Only it wasn't as positive. Sadie didn't display confidence in her abilities as a stage actress, and Ms. Nolan wasn't exactly the cheerleader type. She could still hear the critical tone her old drama coach had in her voice, along with her cutting comment that Sadie didn't have what it took to make it in the theater. Sadie realized far too late that the harsh remark was probably meant to motivate her, yet she took it to heart and it did exactly the opposite. It had changed the course of her life. Years of experience had helped her gain insight. She'd vowed never to crush a student's dreams with a harsh comment. There was a better way to give constructive criticism.

"You're extremely talented, Marla. If you're selected to play this role, you'll have to put your heart in your work and believe in yourself. Of course, we will guide you along the way." She smiled. "You're a natural." She held onto Marla's upper arms and gave a light squeeze. The clatter from backstage reminded her of opening night so many years ago. She raised her hand and rested it on her chest and sighed.

"Thank you, Ms. Lane. If I get the part, I'll work hard. You can count on me." Marla's expression brightened. "I only hope my mother doesn't need me to babysit."

"Is there a problem at home?" Sadie asked curiously.

"No, everything is fine. My mom works in an emergency room, and she needs my help from time to time, but I'll ask my Aunt Suzy to stand by if my mom needs to put in extra hours at work."

"I see. You're a considerate young woman. I'm sure your mother appreciates all you do."

Marla smiled and rushed over to a small gathering at stage left.

Just as Sadie was about to take her place beside the director again, her cellphone buzzed in her pocket. She glanced at the screen and saw it was Vince calling her. "Excuse me. I need to take this." She marched to the back of the room and out into the hallway. Her hands shook. Vince was supposed to be busy all day.

"I called to see how auditions were going," Vince said.

"Very well. How's everything with you?"

"Turn around and you'll find out."

"What?" She nearly fell over as she checked

behind her. "You…you're here?" Her jaw dropped.

He advanced toward her. "I had to come." He took hold of her arms. "I treated you poorly last night, and I want to apologize."

"No—"

"Shh…listen. I wanted desperately to spend the night with you. I was a fool to leave you hanging. Can you forgive me?"

"What about the show and rehearsals?" Her legs wobbled, and she steadied her stance.

"I have time before the rehearsals begin. I have time to give you a hand with the show. If you could use an extra hand that is. It would be like the old days."

Her head spun and her heart filled with joy. "I would like that. I appreciate the offer." She'd hoped he would be able to assist in the production. It would be fun. "Wait until I tell the kids, and Ms. Cartwright." She smiled and took his hand. "Come inside. They're waiting for me."

All eyes were on them when they entered the room. Her face felt warm as an oven.

"I'm sorry to make you all wait. I've got a surprise. This is Vince De Carlo, an old friend from the theater. He's starring in an upcoming Broadway musical, and he's agreed to work with us on this year's show." She put on a big smile.

Vince waved as the students said a hello in unison. She led the way to the stage and being on it together under the bright lights felt like old times. It brought back some of her most treasured memories. Sadie glanced over at Vince and found him staring at her with a boyish grin on his face. It was as if they had gone back in a time machine and were at tryouts themselves.

He'd given her the same supportive smile back then. Her secret crush had blossomed into an adult love affair. Who knew?

"How far along the process have you gotten?" he asked.

"Everyone has read once, and we're about to do second readings. We've got a couple of great prospects." Sadie smiled. She tried to focus, but since he'd arrived, she'd become giddy. She couldn't take her eyes off his smile and the cute little dimple in his chin.

"Great. Let's go," he responded.

"Before we get started, I have to ask you a question." She pulled him off to the side and whispered, "Did I say something to upset you at dinner last night?" Sadie had to get it out in the open if they were going to work together.

"Not at all. What makes you think you did?" Vince asked as he placed his hands in his pockets.

"I know you apologized and you had an early appointment, but I also know you wanted to come in instead of taking off so quick. What was the real reason? Is there someone else?" She took a deep breath, happy to get it out in the open. "It's better to be honest before we get in too deep, if you know what I mean." Sadie glanced over her shoulder to make sure no one was close enough to hear them.

If she had her wish, they'd be back at her place right now. *Why does he have to be so darn sexy?* She hoped she would be able to keep her hands off of him long enough to get through the auditions.

It was hard to stick to her new resolutions. Worry and self-doubt had a way of intruding into her thoughts. It might be time to jot down her affirmations and talk to someone about the reoccurring doubts relating to her career choice. She wished there was a way to turn back the clock. Now that she had a mortgage and a commitment to her students, she couldn't leave it all behind and return to the sometimes unstable life of an actress. She squared her shoulders and held her head high.

"You are an amazing woman, and it was my mistake. I'm here now," he said with sincerity.

"We're about to get started," Sadie said.

The students sat in wooden chairs, waiting for their turn, as the auditions continued. One by one, they read and sang a few bars. Sadie tried her best to stay calm and focused, all the time biting her lip and wondering if she'd see Vince later in the evening. Hot flashes shot through her body like a rapid fire. She was too young for frequent changes in body temperature. Sadie picked up a pitcher from the table, poured herself a glass of iced water, and took a few good-sized sips.

"Are you okay? It is awfully stuffy in here today." Vince moved in closer to her.

"Oh, I'm fine. Just thirsty." She sat back and wiped her neck with a napkin. He probably didn't realize how being with him was affecting her.

After the last student tried out, Ms. Cartwright, Vince, and Sadie put their heads together to make the final decisions. Marla was the forerunner for the female lead, as Sadie had anticipated. Once they'd finished the selections, the announcements were made. Manny Cummings got the male lead and Marla Miles, the female. Hopefully, Marla had found a way to tuck her insecurities aside and go for it. Her talent certainly set her apart. By the sound of the cheers, the celebrations had begun.

Sadie stood. "Congratulations to all, and thank you everyone. The show is going to be a huge hit. If anyone wants to work backstage or help in another way, you are more than welcome."

It was difficult to see the disappointed faces of the pupils who missed the mark on the roles they'd wanted, but most of them did get in the show. Even if they didn't get the parts they'd tried out for, there was enough room for them in the chorus and swing roles.

Vince got up and was quickly surrounded by some of the cast members. Sadie watched as he answered their questions. It was wonderful to see him bask in his glory now that he was a Broadway performer himself. It was perfect timing.

After Sadie thanked Ms. Cartwright and the pianist, the ladies headed out. She and Vince were left to escort the kids out of the auditorium. She remembered how excited they were as teenagers when they had tryouts for a new show. There was nothing that compared to being selected for a role you'd prepared for.

The crowd around Vince finally broke up, and she smiled and walked over to him. "Are you ready?"

He put his arm around her shoulder. "I'm starving. Let's go someplace quiet to grab a bite."

"I know the best little place," she said.

"Oh, you do?" Vince gave her a squeeze.

"Yes, my place." Sadie gave a tiny grin and chuckled.

"Only if you let me make dinner."

"What?" She never knew Vince to be much of a chef.

He snuck a kiss on the cheek. "I grill a mean

steak."

"If you insist, but I'll help."

"It's your night off. I'll take care of everything." He gave her a quick peck on the cheek and took off.

Sadie loved the way he took charge. She'd show him how much she appreciated it after dinner. She found her newly liberated sexuality exciting. Their passion was blossoming, and she wanted to enjoy this phase of discovery with Vince.

Chapter 9

Vince couldn't help but smile on the ride over to Sadie's. He'd hoped she'd invite him to her house. After his stupid move last night, he could have lost her for good. What was he thinking? Things had worked out better than he'd expected. He'd show her how much she meant to him, and he couldn't wait to be alone with her.

With the loan from his father, he'd be able to treat her the way he felt she'd always deserved. He knew all too well that Sadie wasn't the type of girl who demanded exotic vacations, diamonds, or fine dining. Nevertheless, he wanted to be able to take her out, and with his funds near zero, she'd be treating if he hadn't run into his dad. One day, they would be able to look back and laugh at the things they did for love. For now, he'd concentrate on showing her how much she meant to him. With all of the changes in his life in such a short time, he realized how the years of sacrifice had finally paid off. It'd be icing on the cake if his mother and father found a way to work things out.

He drove with one arm resting on the window. The warm air felt great on his skin, and life was finally good.

Sadie had taken her own car home, and he'd meet her, but first he wanted to stop at the store to buy a bottle of wine and a couple of steaks. The grocery store parking lot was practically empty when he pulled in. Vince hopped out and bolted inside. He picked up a basket from the floor and headed straight to the meat aisle. The perfect porterhouses sat in the counter. Vince selected the best package and scooted over to the fresh fruit and vegetables. Once he grabbed the rest of the items for the dinner, he hurried to the express line, and was out the door in minutes. He loaded the bags in his back seat and took off.

He had just enough time to stop at his place for a quick shower. For whatever reason, his luck was going strong. He'd made it through all of the lights without having to stop. At his place, he turned into the pebbled driveway, jumped out of his car, went around to pick up the groceries, and started up the walkway. Inside his apartment, he chucked a few old leftovers in his refrigerator, and stuck the food and wine on the top shelf. He snuck a look at his watch and hurried into the bathroom, shed his clothes, adjusted the water, and stepped into the shower.

The warm water eased some of the tension in his back. He wasn't nervous about preparing dinner for Sadie, but the excitement of a second chance made his pulse kick up a notch. When he was finished, Vince got out, toweled off, and got dressed. He rubbed his hand over his face. There wasn't time for a shave, but he'd remembered how Sadie used to urge him to grow a beard. She'd tease him about a dark-haired man looking sexy with a little stubble. He applied a few sprays of the cologne he'd kept aside for a special night. A night with Sadie was on the top of the list of exceptional occasions.

Vince felt his heart skip a beat as he opened the

fridge and took out the fixings for a romantic dinner with an amazing woman. He glanced at the clock on the microwave and left. Inside his car, he shot a look in his mirror and combed his hair back. This was it.

He drove toward Sadie's house, feeling an adrenaline rush like no other. Nothing was going to stop him. An opportunity to get Sadie back wasn't by coincidence. In his heart, he felt as if they'd always belonged together. He knew it, even back then. Something clicked between them. They'd confessed secrets, their insecurities, and the kiss they'd shared onstage wasn't acting. It was real. His hunch had been validated when he'd made love to her. She'd had the same feelings as he did all along. There wasn't a moment to waste.

He glanced in his rearview mirror and saw his mother driving behind him, motioning for him to stop. Why on earth was his mother waving him over? He didn't want to be late, but he had no choice but to pull over in The Seahorse gift shop parking lot. Funny how a distant memory of when he'd browsed around the tiny store with Sadie one afternoon after rehearsal popped into his head. Hopefully, his mother would understand when he told her he was in a hurry.

He rolled down his window and rested his arm on the car door. His mother parked her car and got out. She ran over to his car.

"What's going on?" he asked. The worried frown on his mother's face concerned him. His gut tightened. She didn't signal him to say hello like he'd thought. Something was terribly wrong. His heart sunk.

"I'm so glad I caught you." She was out of breath. "It…it's your father," she said, her voice shaky. She paused. Was she about to burst out in tears? Her lips lost their color, and her eyes were puffy.

"Mom, are you okay? Was there an accident or something?" He stepped out of the car and put his arm around her. She rested her head on his shoulder and broke down. His heart thumped hard in his chest. His head filled with a string of what if's as he patted her back.

She finally pulled back and gave him a blank stare. "He had crushing chest pain." She pressed her lips together and closed her eyes for a moment. "The doctor transferred him to ICU, and he's set to have an angiogram. They've got him stable for now. It's funny, now that he's clean and sober, this happens." Tears filled her eyes.

"I'm so sorry, but relieved that there's a plan in place to fix it. Did you see him yet?" He felt the perspiration trickle down his forehead, and he reached into his car window, took a napkin from the visor, and wiped his brow.

"Yes, I was by his side. It happened when we were together," she admitted, still trembling.

"Is Dad living back at the house with you?" He met her teary gaze with so many thoughts going through his head.

"I was going to tell you, but we wanted to do it together." She turned her gaze downward.

"I understand." He gently touched her arm. "Get in, I'll drive," Vince insisted. She was too shaken up to be alone.

"No, I'm okay to drive. I'll meet you there. He's at Community," she said as she started to leave.

"I have to drop something off at Sadie's first, but I

won't be long," Vince shouted.

She turned and offered a hesitant grin before she got into her car.

Vince buckled up, gripped the steering wheel, and pushed down on the gas pedal. He took off with his head in a fog. His heart raced. He knew Sadie would understand. His mother needed him, and since he'd reconciled with his father, he wanted to show up and offer his support more than ever. Disappointment and regret tugged at his heart over the many years lost between them. Time certainly didn't wait for anyone.

When he arrived at Sadie's house she was waiting for him at the front door. She greeted him with a big smile and came outside as he parked in the driveway. It broke his heart to have to disappoint her again.

"I was starting to think you got lost," she joked while he got out of his car.

Vince lifted the bags from the back seat, straightened his back, and tried to smile. It wasn't going to be easy, but he knew she'd be supportive.

They went inside, and Sadie hurried into the kitchen with Vince trailing behind. She faced him and crossed her arms with her back up against the granite countertop. "Are you going to tell me what happened?" Soft listening music played on the stereo in her living room.

She knew him all too well. Vince swallowed hard before he spoke. He feared for his father's health, and his heart ached for his parents.

"I won't be able to stay and prepare dinner." He paused and his gaze hit the floor.

He clenched his fist with the knot in his stomach worsening. He was worried about his father. Vince looked directly at her. "My father had a heart attack. I saw my mother on the road, and she flagged me down and told me what happened. I need to go to the hospital." He flicked a strand of hair off of his forehead.

"I'm so sorry, Vince. Do you want me to go with you?" She rushed to his side and gave him a comforting hug.

"That is so sweet of you, however, I think it'd be better if you stay here. He's in ICU, and the visitors may be restricted." Vince pulled her close and stroked her back.

She stepped back and gave him a sympathetic stare. "Please keep me updated, and I'll be right here if you need me. I'm praying for him," she said with sincerity.

"Okay. Thank you." He gave her another hug and left.

****

The doorbell rang and Sadie rushed to answer it, wondering if Vince had forgotten something. Instead, Millie and Jill stood on her doorstep. She welcomed them inside. "Hi, you two. How did you know I was by myself?"

"We were passing by and saw Vince leaving. Carol Mitchell lives down the street and we picked up our orders from her jewelry party. Remember, you didn't want to come?" Jill said as she walked into the living room and plopped on the sofa.

Millie followed and sat in an arm chair.

"You missed out on some pretty things. You can borrow mine if you'd like," Jill added.

Sadie sat next to Jill.

"Did you have an argument or something? It's still

early." Jill crossed her legs.

"Vince was on his way over to grill a couple of steaks for us when he saw his mother and she told him that his father is in the hospital. It's his heart. So Vince had to go to the hospital to check on him."

"I'm sorry about his father. I hope he's going to pull through."

"Oh, my goodness! How awful. I hope he's okay," Millie joined in.

"Thank you, both of you." Sadie looked down, her anticipation unsettling. Hopefully, Mr. De Carlo would be okay.

"So how are you getting along?" Jill sat forward.

"We're doing fine. He's a great guy."

"By the color of your cheeks and the lovey tone in your voice, I can tell you're falling in love with him. Am I wrong?"

"Give her a break," Millie said. "You don't have to answer if you don't want to, Sadie. We're happy for you, that's all."

"I didn't say we weren't happy. I want the sizzling details," Jill demanded.

Sadie sat back and placed her hands in her lap, feeling like she may as well confess. "I am falling hard for Vince. I might even say the L word."

"I knew it!"

Millie grinned. "That's great. I know you had a thing in the past, or an almost thing."

"We were too young, and I was focused on my career. I'm ready now." She shifted her position.

"He's a dynamite lover, right?" Jill blurted.

"None of your business." She held her lips tight. "Magical is all I have to say."

"I bet he is." Jill shook her head, wearing a grin. She stood. "We better get out of here before we ruin your chances of getting lucky."

"You've got one thing on your mind, Jill," Millie insisted and stood.

"I'm the only one who tells it like it is. It's my way of saying I love you."

"I know. I appreciate your honesty. I'll walk with you. I'm glad you stopped by." Sadie got up and followed them.

They went outside. Sadie inhaled the sweet scent of her spring mix on her porch. "I'll call you. We have to have lunch together on the weekend. Maybe we'll go to the outlets. I could use a new purse."

"Okay. That's sounds like a plan." Jill got in the driver's seat.

Sadie watched until they were out of sight, and then she went back inside.

It was merely minutes after she closed the door, and the doorbell rang again. She opened the door and was surprised to see her mother standing there. Why was her mother there? Sadie welcomed her with a hug. Her mother was a tall, slender woman, and she always wore clothes that gave Sadie a sense that she'd just stepped out of Woodstock. Her long, flowing skirt and pleasant blouse looked pretty.

"I won't stay but a minute." She stepped inside and went into the living room.

Sadie joined her.

"I'm going to a Rocky Horror Show viewing at the old Royal Theater with your Aunt Loretta." She eyed Sadie up and down. "I love you, and I know you have been through so much in your life. All I know is, you're well, and I don't want you to limit yourself. Go for the life you deserve, and never look back. In every area of your life. You hear me?"

Sadie raised her hand to her neck and a chill rattled her body. "Mom, do you want to sit? I'll make you a quick cup of tea."

"I don't have time. If I don't get going, I'm going to be late. But I can tell you have something on your mind. You've got that sparkle in your eyes. Like the time you got the role in Grease. Is there something you want to tell me?"

"I'm in love with Vince De Carlo, from my old theater group. We got together in LA. I have so much to tell you." Her whole body relaxed. The realization of her feelings for Vince hit her hard, especially after confessing it to her mother.

Her mother's smile brightened her face. "I'm thrilled. I knew you two would get together one day." She reached for Sadie's arm and peeked over her wire-rimmed glasses. "I spoke with Mrs. De Carlo. Mothers stick together. We're so happy for you both."

"Thanks, Mom."

"I'm going to have you both over, and Vince's mother and father. That is if they're still together. The last time I spoke to Mary, she'd thrown him out. Poor thing. She is such a good woman. She mentioned they recently reconciled though."

"I believe they're on good terms. His father had a medical emergency today and he's in the hospital."

"That's terrible. Hope it's nothing serious. I pray he'll be okay. Let me know."

"I will. I promise."

"I wish I could stay, but I have to run. I'll call you

tomorrow. Remember what I said." She gave Sadie a kiss on the forehead and another big hug.

Sadie closed the door and practically floated into the kitchen. She'd confessed her feelings, and it felt great.

****

Vince arrived at the hospital pretty quickly since the traffic wasn't bad. He rushed through the parking deck and pushed the door to the main entrance. Up at the information desk, a woman smiled. He told him who he was there to see, and she handed him a pass.

The fourth floor housed a huge intensive care unit. He picked up the phone next to the wall to announce himself. Inside, he was guided by a friendly, young male nurse, who whispered the time limit on visits. Only fifteen minutes at a time.

He took a few deep breaths and joined his mother at his father's bedside. Luckily, his dad was breathing on his own. His color was pink and he was awake. A good sign. Vince went over and sat next to the bed, placing his hand on top of his father's.

His dad smiled. "Thank you for coming, Vince."

"How do you feel?"

"I'm much better. The procedure went well. The pain is gone. I'm a new man in every possible way. I've got to remain flat for a while longer."

"That's great. What happened? You looked fine when I last saw you."

"Looks are deceiving. Years of hard living and abusing my body finally caught up to me." He coughed. "I'm one lucky man." He nodded toward Vince's mom. "If it wasn't for your mom, I might not be here. She insisted on calling the ambulance when I told her I had discomfort in my chest and felt lightheaded. They wheeled me right into the cardiac lab, and I'm fixed."

The beeping of the cardiac monitor when his dad moved made him a little edgy. His hands shook. "Yes, she cares about you. I'm glad you sought help right away." Vince nodded, amazed at how well his father seemed to be taking it. He'd morphed into a different person, more stable and accepting, despite his sudden illness.

His father glanced at his wife and gave her a loving grin.

"Did the doctor say anything else?" Vince crossed his legs, feeling a deep sense of gratitude in his heart. "It could have been so much worse."

"Vince was on his way to see Sadie Layne when I pulled him over to tell him what had happened," his mother announced.

"I'm okay now. Don't leave Sadie waiting another minute. You have to grasp on tight. Don't miss out on second chances. Believe me, I know how to mess up a good thing." His father chuckled and cleared his throat as he reached for his wife's hand.

They'd been through horrific times together, and despite this setback, they looked happier than ever.

Vince grinned and realized the message his dad was relaying. "Are you sure you're okay?"

"I'm better than ever. Believe me."

"Okay. I'm out of here. Thank you, Dad. Get some rest. I'm happy you feel better." He stood. "Are you staying for a while, Mom?"

"Yes, I want to speak with the doctor. Go on." She smiled.

Vince went over and gave his mother a hug. "Call

me if you need me. I'll be here in a flash." He moved to his father's bed and gave him a goodbye hug. It felt great to be a family again, and even through a medical scare, he held on to a sense of hope for his parents' future.

Maybe he'd still have time to make it up to Sadie. He'd whip up a late dinner, if she hadn't already made new plans.

****

Sadie read a text from Vince. What good news. His father was doing well.

She slipped her cellphone in her apron picket, picked up a fork, and turned the steaks. She'd found a recipe for a spice rub on the internet. She'd prepared the kale-arugula blend salad and put it in the refrigerator. Vince had already left the hospital. He'd be there in about thirty minutes. She set the table for two. There was time to finish the last minute touches and freshen up before he arrived. Her stomach growled as she placed the meat on a plate, shut the propane off, and carried the food inside. Hopefully, she'd cooked them just right. The grill wasn't her specialty.

It only took a few minutes for the rolls to heat up. With the bread toasty and tucked into a basket, she went into the bathroom to get ready. It'd be fun to surprise Vince. He'd been through enough this evening. She couldn't wait to see his face when he walked in and saw the table set and the food prepared. He'd be able to make dinner another night. She stood at the head of the table with a sense of pride in her heart and the light fluttering in her stomach.

She heard him pull up, hurried to the door, and quickly opened it. Judging by the weary look on

Vince's face, she knew she'd done the right thing. He'd never hold up. As soon as he got inside, she wrapped her arms around him and gave a squeeze. "I'm happy it worked out okay. You must be exhausted."

"I am." Vince sighed and took her hand as they went into the kitchen. "I may be tired, but I can throw the meal together in a few minutes," he insisted.

"There's no need to cook."

"What?" He gave her a leery look.

"I already grilled and the table is set." She gave him a happy grin, pleased to take the burden off of him.

"I thought I smelled garlic. You're an angel. I'm so hungry, I'm about to keel over."

She slid her arm through his and ushered Vince into the dining room.

"This is unbelievable." He turned to face her and put his hands on the sides of her face, before placing his lips gently on hers.

Sadie stood on her toes, and when the kiss ended, she felt a little tipsy. She rested her hand on the table. "Sit here."

"No, ladies first." He pulled out her chair, and she gazed up at him, and sat.

"Thank you."

Vince sat across from her and opened his napkin. He poured Sadie a glass of wine and then one for himself. "This looks delicious." He cut his steak and sampled it. "You're a great grill chef."

"It was beginner's luck." She took a bite. "It is good." She sipped her wine. "Did you get the details on your father's illness?"

"Yes, he was lucky. He's finished with the angiogram, and he's doing well." He took a deep breath. "Overall, he's feeling much better. I felt bad for him. As soon as things are going well, bingo…illness strikes."

"Tell me about it. I thought I had years before I'd even need a specialist, if I ever did. You never know when things will change. That's why I changed my philosophy. No more waiting to enjoy my life." She raised her glass in the air.

"To making each day count." Vince joined her in the toast. "After seeing my father tonight, it really hit me. I'm so fortunate to have you back in my life, and I'm over-the-top ecstatic that I scored the steady gig on Broadway. I only hope the show pulls in the crowds." He buttered a piece of bread and took a bite.

"I'm so proud of you, Vince. I know you'll be great in the role." Even though she encouraged him, her regrets wouldn't quit. She still had the bug to perform. Why not admit it and move forward? Sadie downed the rest of her wine.

"Do you want another glass?"

"Sure, fill it up."

"Okay, but we have rehearsals tomorrow, and you have class in the morning. Not that I'm telling you what to do." He gave a wink. "I'm staying over, if you don't mind."

"Of course I want you to stay the night." Sadie couldn't wait until dinner was over. His familiar, sensual, earthy cologne had hit her as soon as he'd walked in, and she longed for his gentle caress.

After they finished dinner, she pushed her plate away. The bamboo and lily candle in the middle of the table flickered, giving a soft hue to the room, and she caught his gaze. Vince reached for her hand and ran his thumb in circles up her wrist and to her forearm, sending shivers through her body. His loving gesture was discrete, but it was just what she needed. She was crazy about this man, and despite her fears, she couldn't resist one more minute.

"I'll help you clear the table." Vince stood and gathered the dishes and silverware.

They went into the kitchen.

"I'll give you a hand," Vince said.

"I'm going to let the dishwasher do the work, but you can help."

"Sounds good to me."

She rinsed the dishes and silverware before handing them to Vince. Vince loaded the last piece in the rack and closed the door.

"Do you want to wait until morning to turn it on?" he asked.

"Sure. I have plenty of dishes. Go ahead and get comfy. I'll be right out." Sadie rushed into her room and to her bathroom to brush her teeth. When she came back out, Vince had changed the station on the stereo to the music they'd listened to when they'd practiced on weekends. A love song she hadn't heard in years took her back to a time long ago.

Sadie found him positioned on the couch with his head resting on the overstuffed pillows. His eyes were half-closed, his arms crossed over his chest. Vince quickly aroused when she made her grand entrance. Sadie swayed back and forth in front of him, until he grabbed her wrist and pulled her gently onto his lap.

"Come here, you sexy woman."

She sat on his lap, and he buried his head in her chest. Sadie stroked the back of his hair, her longing taking control. Vince slowly ran his hand up and down her arm and over to her breast. Her nipples swelled, and as she moved around, she felt his shaft grow in size. Sadie gave a soft moan as he slid his hand under her dress. There was no turning back. Each fiber in her body came alive. Her juices flowed as he gently caressed all of her forbidden places. Her desire for him grew stronger and stronger. He traced her lips with his finger and nibbled at her lips before he darted his tongue deep inside her mouth. Vince's warm breath against her face tantalized her. With his heart pounding next to hers, she came alive. More alive than she'd been in years. Being close to the man she loved was absolute heaven.

"I love you, Sadie." The words came out of his mouth as if he'd said them every day. "I'm sorry, sweetie. I couldn't help it. My love for you began long ago, and it seems as natural as breathing."

His declaration of love and sincerity brought tears to her eyes. Sadie drew a breath in as she tried to hold back the waterfall. "Vince, I feel the same for you. I love you too. This time around, my feelings are clear and I couldn't be happier that we have found each other again."

Vince's expression brightened as she moved over to the side. He stood, scooped her up into his arms, and carried her into the bedroom. He smoothly lowered her to the bed and placed his arms on each side of her. "I'm going to show you how much you mean to me, my precious angel."

"Oh, are you?" She parted her lips and placed her hand on his chest. Sadie's heart told her to hold on tight and appreciate this caring and giving man.

While he undressed her, he kept his gaze fixed on her and traced his mouth with his tongue. He hurried to undress. He gently climbed on top of her, offering soft butterfly kisses from her lips down to her stomach. Each light touch made her body temperature rise. Her hips gyrated as he slowly lifted her legs and entered her. She wanted every inch of him. His hot body, firm and moist, melted into hers, setting her groin on fire. He rotated his hips as he lifted her buttocks, gaining a deeper entrance.

She yelled aloud. "Ah, ah, oh, Vince."

"You're so wet," Vince said, his tone low and breathy.

She puckered her lips and reached up for him, circling his broad chest with her fingers, and then running them down his firm biceps. Their lips met in a fiery connection, with Vince plunging his tongue deeper and deeper inside her mouth. With each hoarse moan he uttered, she came closer to another moment of ecstasy. His strong hands moving desperately all over her body made her feel loved and appreciated. Her heart raced with each thrust. He tenderly nuzzled her neck. His hot skin close to her ear sent a riveting chill throughout her body.

"I can't get enough of you." His hair fell onto his forehead as he lifted his chest.

"You're driving me wild, Vince." Sadie screamed in sheer delight, her heart racing.

She thought she'd faint from the intensity. This was what she'd always wanted, and she never wanted to let him go. When love was the driving force, it brought the connection to a deeper level.

"You do things to me that are out of my control,"

he whispered in her ear.

Her fingers dug deep into his back as he pushed hard, rotating around and around. The room closed in around them. The only thing she could see was Vince. She loved to feel his racing heart next to hers. "Don't stop. Please!"

"Oh, baby. Let go, go on." He pumped harder until they both shook. Screams of pleasure filled the room. As she lay beside him, her body still jerked.

He positioned himself beside her and draped one leg over hers. Sadie stared up at the ceiling and rejoiced for a second chance at life and love. Never in her life did she feel the way she did when Vince held her in his arms. It was as if everything she'd ever wanted in a man was finally within her reach.

"Are you happy?" Vince snuggled close and caressed her belly.

"I'm happier than I've ever been."

"So am I. Who'd ever believe me if I told them I made the cut for Broadway and found my lost love all in the same month?" he proclaimed. "I'm afraid if I blink it will all disappear." He trailed his fingers down the side of her face and to her chest. Each touch set her skin aflame.

"I know. I'm still in a daze over everything happening so fast." She took a deep breath. "I've always had faith in your talent. Hard work pays off. Right?" She closed her eyes and tried to stop herself from reliving past regrets over her stupid decision to leave the theater. Then she remembered her promise to live each day as if it were her last. She wasn't going to let her silly thoughts ruin this wonderful evening.

"Before you know it, I'll be in the theatre for

rehearsals. Wait until you hear the music. Maybe one day I'll arrange for you to visit and go behind the scenes. I could use your honest critique." He faced her and his lips curled up into a charming grin.

She hesitated as she ran her tongue along the bottom of her mouth. "Sure, that'd be wonderful." Sadie's jaw tightened as her voice cracked. She cleared her throat. She'd do anything to rid herself of the same old nagging regrets.

****

The next morning Sadie opened her eyes to the sun filtering in through the white sheers in her bedroom. She'd forgotten to close the shades. She stretched, feeling peaceful and rested. When she snuck a peek at Vince, his eyes were still closed. He looked so content curled up in her bed. Not wanting to wake him, she lifted the sheet and slowly crept out of bed.

In the bathroom, she tried to be as quiet as possible. She slipped on her peach colored, silky robe and started toward the kitchen to prepare two cups of coffee. It was early enough to serve him a light breakfast in bed. The school was close enough for her to get there in less than ten minutes, a definite perk of working close to home. Sadie might have it tough with time management if she had to commute. She liked to stay up late and catch her favorite movies on television. The glamour of old Hollywood had always held her interest.

She remembered how Vince took his coffee, and she knew he'd munch on a chocolate chip protein bar. They used to stop at McFarland's neighborhood store and grab a few for extra energy. Sadie placed the bars and coffee on a pretty turquoise serving tray she got for a house warming present from her mother and carried it into the bedroom. As she set it down on the dresser, Vince stirred.

"Good morning, beautiful," he greeted.

"You're up, sleepyhead." She picked up the tray and brought it over to the bed.

Vince propped the pillows behind his back. "What's this?"

She set the breakfast down next to him and crawled in bed beside him. "I made us a little treat. Do you remember these?" Sadie held up the package.

"I can't believe you found those. I've been looking all over for them. The grocery store doesn't carry them anymore."

"Silly, have you tried the place we used to get them from?"

"No, where was that?"

"McFarland's on Third Avenue." She smiled.

"You amaze me with your attention to details. I guess I was too focused on you back then." He placed his hand on top of hers.

"I remembered how you like your coffee too. Not too light, two sugars."

He picked up the cup and took a sip. "I'm impressed. Thank you." He gave her an adoring grin. "You're not only gorgeous, talented, and sexy, you can cook and you remember the little things. How did I get so lucky? What are you doing with a nut like me?" he joked and tickled her lightly.

She rested her arm on the bed. "In this case, opposites don't attract. We're a lot alike," she quickly returned.

"You got me there." He opened the protein bar and

took a bite. "Hmm." He held the bar up. "It's great to have you back." Vince took another bite.

"You are a little nutty, but so am I."

"You're right." He laughed.

"You don't have to agree." Sadie munched on the chocolatey treat and finished her cup of coffee. "That was so good. I could go for another, but I'm jumping into the shower. Do you want to join me?"

Before he could answer, Sadie's cellphone rang. "Who on earth?" She picked up the call.

Marla, her student on the other end, was difficult to understand.

"Calm down. I can't understand you. Now, take a slow, deep breath." She got up and went into the other room. Sadie motioned to Vince that she'd be right back. It was better to speak to her student in private. "What's making you so upset?"

"I'm not taking the role. I've made up my mind. It is too much for me. I'm not ready." Marla broke down.

"I know it's a huge undertaking, and it requires commitment, but you are capable of this. I'm sure of it. Did something happen to make you change your mind?"

It took a moment for Marla to answer, and Sadie worried that she may have had a more serious issue at home. She nervously straightened the magazines on her coffee table.

"Well, the other students have been asking me how I got the part instead of Carolyn. I can't take the pressure. Maybe you should give her the role instead. I'll be in the chorus, or I'll take another role."

Sadie paced around her living room as she gripped her phone tight. The challenges of life at Marla's age weren't unfamiliar to Sadie. She knew all too well how it took a different level of maturity to feel comfortable and self-assured. "I realize peer pressure is hard to handle. This is your chance, Marla. Jackie Kale, the talent scout, promised to attend opening night. You can't let the others steal this opportunity. We'll talk more about it later. I'm here for you, don't ever forget that."

"It's nice of you to listen to me complain. I'm sorry to give you a problem," Marla responded.

"You're not giving me a problem. I'm your teacher, and I care about each and every one of my students. Are you going to be okay until I see you? We can work together. Maybe on the weekends."

"I guess I'll be okay. I do feel much better after talking to you. I really want this role. I've already memorized my lines."

"Good for you." Sadie heard a tone of confidence in her reply. "Hold your head high. You can do this."

"Thank you, Miss Layne. I'll see you later."

Sadie went back into the bedroom and over to Vince. She sat beside him on the bed. "I'm sorry. It was Marla, the girl we chose for the lead. I had to give her a pep talk. Oh, do I remember how tough it is when you're her age."

It felt great to be there for her student. She'd almost forgotten how important a mentor can be, and also how a negative remark or interpretation of one can affect a young life. She'd done exactly that when she was a teenager. If she'd only had a supportive mentor. Her mother had tried, but Sadie wouldn't listen. "Parents don't understand" was her philosophy at the time. She relaxed her shoulders.

Kathleen Ann Gallagher

"It's a good thing she has you to talk to," Vince replied as he gently rubbed her back.

"Yes, I'm happy to be there for my students. I've got to get ready quickly. I remembered something I have to do at school before class. Do you mind if I take a raincheck on our shower?" She tilted her head and gave him a hint of a grin.

"You do what you have to. I understand. Anyway, I want to run home to shower and stop by to see my father. I can catch up with you later at practice." Vince got up and put on his pants. Then he went over to Sadie and took her by the shoulders. "I haven't slept that good since I was a kid. You make me so happy." He gave her a soft kiss as he ran his strong fingers through the back of her hair, sending shivers down to her feet.

****

Vince finished getting dressed, and Sadie gave him the cutest grin. He picked up his phone and keys from the side table. "I'll call you when I'm on my way to the school," he added.

He held her close and gave her one last tender kiss before he left. Deep in his gut, doubt over taking the relationship to the next level worried him. It meant nights spent at the theater, promotion, days apart, and the main thing was waiting for him to pursue his dream. Could he have both his career and the woman he loved? It seemed like a tall order. Yet his heart flipped every time he touched her. Vince had the utmost respect for Sadie, he always did. Was it the time for them?

Vince drove home singing along with the radio, and after he got in and showered, he stumbled across an old movie ticket tucked in a corner of the top drawer of his dresser. It must have been stuck in between some

196

papers when he unpacked. He held it up to the light. It was from the night the whole bunch of them from the workshop went on an outing after tryouts. Sadie was by his side that night. He recalled how his hands shook all through the movie, and the funny way she'd nudged him during the scary scenes. When she'd put her head on his shoulder to hide her eyes, he'd almost jumped for joy. Last night she'd declared her love for him, and deep in his heart, he always believed she'd be back.

He left for the hospital with so many different thoughts twirling around in his head. It made him happy when his mother expressed her happiness over Sadie and him getting together, and it was nice to be able to share his feelings with her. She seemed more understanding since she'd been in therapy and his father had found recovery. This medical emergency wasn't going to stop them. Their love was strong, and together they'd make it through this. Seeing what his parents went through and how their love sustained the awful grips of addiction made him realize how strong their love was. He let go of his resentments and even felt a twinge of guilt over the way he'd treated his dad.

It was as if he grew up over the past few days. It wasn't fair to keep Sadie hanging in the wings as he committed to a Broadway show, and who knew where afterward. He was being selfish, and it wasn't the time to play games. A long-term relationship wasn't something he knew how to do. His heart broke to think of Sadie's face if he told her goodbye. If it wasn't the right time for them now, then when was it? His indecision was messing him up. *Maybe this is what happens when you're in love.* He wanted her, but didn't want to have to ask her to be patient until his career was stable.

His father was up and sitting in the bedside chair when he arrived. The nurse at the station told Vince it was all right to visit. When he stood at the door, he couldn't believe how good his dad looked. His face had a healthy glow, and he was up eating lunch as if nothing had happened.

"Hey, you look like you're on a vacation instead of being in the hospital," he said, his voice strong.

"The doc fixed me up good. Didn't he?" He glanced over at his wife and nodded.

"Dad can come home later this afternoon. Thank goodness his heart is strong. He was very fortunate. He's going to be okay. The doctor is giving him a prescription for a cardiac medication and a cholesterol pill. With a change in diet and a rehab a couple times of week, he'll be better than ever." She sounded as happy as a young bride.

"Do you need anything?" Vince sat in a bedside chair.

"Nope. I have everything I need right here in this room."

"I suppose you do."

"How was your date with Sadie?" he asked.

"We had a great time. She is really special." He smiled. Vince couldn't hide the way he felt about Sadie. If only he didn't feel so guilty making her wait.

"I'm happy for you, both of you." His dad offered an accepting grin. "Son, you go after what you want, and don't waste time worrying." He gave Vince an intense look.

"What's wrong?"

"You tell me."

"Umm…nothing is wrong."

"Since you're having this little father-to-son, I'm going down for a cup of coffee." His mom left the room.

"I know that look. We all question the way we feel when we find the right woman. You know deep in your gut what you have to do. Don't mess with fate. Time doesn't wait for anyone. Your mother and I are back together because she believed in our love, and I made up my mind to never take her for granted again. God, I wasted precious years." He looked up at the ceiling and brought his hands together as if to pray.

"I don't want you worrying about me, Dad. I hear everything you're saying." Vince was amazed at his father's change and positive attitude, but he knew the old man was a wise man.

"I mean every word. Don't leave that young lady alone for too long."

He was right. Love wasn't ideal, but Sadie was the best thing that ever happened to him. There wasn't anything he couldn't do with her by his side. He took a deep breath and realized how foolish he'd been to even think of losing her again.

Vince checked his watch. "Sorry, I can't stay longer. I have someplace to be."

"You get the hell out of here and go for it all. You hear me?"

"Are you going to be okay?"

"Don't worry. I'm in good hands." He pointed upward.

"Tell Mom I'll talk to her later, and call me if you need anything." He got up and turned to leave, but glanced back over his shoulder at his father with a sense of peace in his heart.

Vince almost forgot he had to shoot over to see his agent. He'd have to put it in gear.

Once he'd arrived at the office, his faithful manager had the papers prepared and ready. Vince wasn't surprised when Joey stuck in a few pokes about how he seemed like a love-struck kid.

"It is great to be young and in love." Joey tipped his cap. "Was I ever your age?"

"It is hard to believe. I'm late. Sorry I have to hurry." Vince rubbed his chin as he stood in front of Joey's desk.

"You don't have to agree with me. Now, get out of here. Your lady is waiting."

As he drove back to his apartment, the few clouds overhead had disappeared. The temperature was warm for this time of year, and he drove with the windows open. The scent of the ocean air was refreshing. Vince parked in front and rushed inside. He stripped and changed into a dark washed pair of jeans and a black t-shirt. He took the short cut and arrived only a couple of minutes late.

****

Sadie was already in the auditorium when Vince arrived. The students held their scripts tight in their hands.

He waved to Sadie. "Did I miss anything?" he asked.

"Not a thing. We've been waiting for you." She stepped down from the stage and glided over to greet him.

"How is Miss Marla holding up?"

"You know, it was wonderful to be able to offer

her guidance. She took my advice and she needed it, believe me. Vince, I'm exactly where I'm supposed to be." Pride filled her spirit.

"I agree." He squinted. "Are you telling me everything?"

She moved closer. "I have to confess. I've had my doubts about my decision to leave the theater, and after hearing about your Broadway role, I started really doubting myself." She sighed.

"I had no idea. I'm so sorry to make you feel that way." He held onto her arm.

"No, no, you had nothing to do with it. It was all in my head. I thought I had it resolved years ago, I guess I was still unsure. I do love teaching, and this thing with Marla... I don't know, it reached inside and helped me realize where I need to stay. I can make a difference here, and it's essential for the young people of today to have positive role models and mentors. Right here with my students is my home." She put on a happy face.

"That's wonderful. You're a great teacher. You make a difference, and they need you."

"Thanks." She fluttered her eyelashes. "By the way, how is your father?"

"He's doing well, and he's being discharged today. Dad is where he belongs too—with my mother. It looks like there are two happily reunited couples in Point Pleasant Beach." He took her in his arms and held her close, and then he gave her a quick peck on the lips. "I love you with all of my heart, Sadie. I always have."

Sadie glanced up at the stage and laughed when she noticed the whole group of students lined up applauding. Vince pulled her closer and chuckled along with her. Her face was warm and felt tingly, but inside her heart she'd found purpose, with no reservations or second-guessing. She'd tucked her desires deep inside and never faced them head-on, however, teaching was her calling. Her doubts had finally cleared.

Now, with Vince by her side and back in her life, she'd never let a day go by without telling him how much she loved him. He put his arm around her shoulders and together they started toward the stage.

"We have lot of work to do before opening night. Are you ready?" Vince gave Sadie's arm a gentle squeeze and pulled her close.

"I've never been more ready in my life."

A word about the author...

Kathleen lived in NJ prior to relocating to Florida with her husband and their fur baby Luc. When she is not writing or reading, she enjoys spending time at the beach collecting shells, taking long walks, and spending time with her four grandsons. Kathleen also performs in community theater in Southwest Fl.

Thank you for purchasing
this publication of The Wild Rose Press, Inc.

For questions or more information
contact us at
info@thewildrosepress.com.

The Wild Rose Press, Inc.
www.thewildrosepress.com